EDEN
WEST

EDEN WEST

PETE HAUTMAN

CANDLEWICK PRESS

For the Anfinson boys

Copyright © 2015 by Pete Hautman
Case illustration copyright © 2015 by Dadu Shin

First edition 2015

Library of Congress Catalog Card Number 2014945452
ISBN 978-0-7636-7418-2

15 16 17 18 19 20 BVG 10 9 8 7 6 5 4 3 2 1

Printed in Berryville, VA, U.S.A.

This book was typeset in Granjon.

Candlewick Press
99 Dover Street
Somerville, Massachusetts 02144

visit us at www.candlewick.com

The wicked surround us when the vile are exalted.

— *Psalm 12*

1

And the Lord of the sheep went with them, as their leader, and all His sheep followed Him.

—Enoch 89:22

1

I know that the World is a terrible place, filled with wild animals and evil men and wicked women. I know that the Beast stalks the streets of the cities, and the canyons and footpaths beyond, and that only the strongest and wisest of men can resist his seductive ways. I know that the End Days are coming.

I know that the Lord will visit His wrath upon this World, and that all who remain are doomed to pay a terrible price, for as their fathers have sinned, so sin their sons. I know this day will soon come upon us.

I know how fortunate I am to be of the Grace, G'bless, and my parents, G'bless, and Father Grace himself, G'bless, and the Archangel Zerachiel, who needs not *my* blessing for he is himself the Lord's Command. And I know that His light shines upon Nodd, and that Zerachiel will come to carry us away from the horrors and pain of the End Days. I know that the Ark will come.

The Day will come, and the Ark will come.

The Ark will come.

The Tree grows in the Sacred Heart of the Village. Brother Benedict and Brother Jerome tend it now, examining the leaves and bark for signs of infestation or disease. To tend the Tree is a great privilege.

I kneel, my knees fitting into depressions worn in the hard soil by other Grace's knees. I rest my elbows on the smooth top of the stone wall that surrounds the Tree, and I think how wondrous a thing it must be to tread upon those roots and upon the fallen fruit, to be trusted so by Father Grace, by Zerachiel, by the Lord Himself. In nine short months, I will have eighteen summers, and I will become a Higher Cherub like Benedict and Jerome. Perhaps one day Father Grace will allow me this honor as well.

The Tree itself is a gnarly, ancient thing, its knotted trunk bigger around than Father Grace's belly, its three main limbs as thick as his thighs. It is as wide as it is tall, arms corkscrewing out from the trunk, sprouting uncountable leafy branchlets, reaching almost to the wall, which is itself thirty cubits across.

It is morning now; sunlight grazes the uppermost leaves of the Tree. A pair of jays alight noisily to peck at the ripe fruit. Brother Jerome rattles the leaves with his staff. Startled, the jays take flight. Leaves fall to the earth.

I close my eyes and whisper all one hundred eight lines of the Arbor Prayer. When I get to the last line—*and the Fruit, and the Lord, and the Ark will come*—I open my eyes to find that I have been joined at the wall by several other Grace whispering their own morning devotions. I touch myself with the sign of the Tree and leave the wall to report to Archcherub Brother Enos. Today is second Landay.

Today, it is my privilege to patrol the borders of Nodd.

I walk the edge on the second and fourth Landays of the month. Brother Will performs the duty on alternate Landays. We patrol our borders to keep our land pure, to protect ourselves from the evils that lie beyond.

Nodd covers 7,800 acres. Much of the land is steep and forested, but there is sufficient grazing land for five score sheep and a small herd of milk cows, and enough tillable land for our crops. The fence, eight-foot chain-link with loops of razor wire coiling along the top, is more than thirteen miles long. It takes the better part of a day to walk it.

In the spring and fall, when the weather is fine, to walk the fence is a pleasure. On this warm September day, I follow the well-trodden path at a leisurely pace, stopping frequently to look out over rolling hills dotted with juniper and sage.

The world beyond the fence is deceptively peaceful looking. The grass is shorter; the landscape crisscrossed by cattle trails. I see them in the distance, scattered groups of twenty or fewer, each beast branded with the mark of the Rocking K Ranch, our neighbor to the north. The cattle often walk close along the fence line; you can see bits of their coarse hair caught on the chain-link. They hope to find a way into our fertile land. Only rarely do we glimpse the Worldly men of the Rocking K. Though they be sinners all, they forbear to trespass upon us.

The south of Nodd borders upon the godless Fort Landreau Indian Reservation. The elders of this Lamanite tribe have agreed to respect our borders. Even so, a year ago some of their young men chose to trespass upon us, cutting through the chain-link to poach our pronghorn and mule deer. Brother John discovered the cold and ugly remains of one of their camps, all ashes and gut piles. I pray that I never stumble upon such a scene.

The river Pison, fast and treacherous, forms our western border. There is no fence, only the water, and it is there that the wild creatures may come and go at will.

There, I laid eyes upon the wolf.

It was late last winter, bitter cold and blowing as only Zerachiel himself can blow. The sky was bright blue, the land covered with drifts of crystalline snow, fine and sharp. Now and again gusts of wind tore at the drifts to send clouds of ice particles swirling through the air. Walking north along the Pison, shards of blowing ice and snow cutting at me, I was thinking irreverent thoughts about Brother Enos for sending me out on such a day. Every few minutes, the blowing snow would come so hard I had to stop and pull my hood over my face and wait for the ground storm to subside.

The Pison herself was nearly frozen; a rare event. A jagged channel about ten cubits across showed black and wet near the center of the river. I was wiping ice from my eyes when I saw the dog sitting at the edge of the ice on the far side of the channel.

Except it wasn't a dog. It had a wildness to it. A coyote, I thought. I unslung my carbine, knelt in the snow, and aimed. The creature was a good three hundred cubits off. I did not trust myself to make the shot at that distance. The carbine is a small rifle, and mine was not mounted with a scope. I would have to wait. Should it choose to cross into Nodd, I would send the beast to Zerachiel.

A fresh gust of wind kicked up another cloud of ice particles, and for several seconds I was blinded by the mini-blizzard. When the snow settled, I saw that the creature was in motion, trotting along the edge of the channel. I knew in that instant, seeing those long legs and the proud tilt of its head, that this was no coyote. It was a wolf.

As if sensing my thoughts, the wolf stopped and looked directly at me, or so it seemed. It sank back on its haunches and leaped, its long gray body stretching out, impossibly long, sailing over the open water for what seemed like seconds, dropping soft as a shadow upon Nodd's ice. It trotted casually up the sloped bank and stopped not fifty cubits away. Again, I raised the carbine to my shoulder.

The wolf looked at me, and this time I was sure he saw

7

me. His tongue showed and his mouth curved into a canine laugh. I released the safety and sighted in on his body, his chest, his heart. My breath came ragged and harsh. I fought to control my breathing. We Cherubim are well trained in the use of firearms. A shot taken in haste is a shot wasted. I willed my pulse to slow. The wolf laughed, his eyes locked upon me. My finger touched the cold steel of the trigger. *Two more slow breaths,* I told myself—but I had waited too long. The wolf became a gray blur, kicking up snow, instantly reaching pronghorn speed and disappearing into a stand of juniper. I never fired.

I returned to the Village, shaking with cold and excitement, and reported what I had seen. Brother Enos questioned me at length. It was clear that he doubted my eyes. "A coyote can look much larger than it is, Brother Jacob, especially when one is alone."

"I saw what I saw," I said. No one in living memory had seen a wolf in Nodd. There are wolves in Yellowstone, but that is hundreds of miles away.

Despite his doubts, Enos promised to send Jerome the next morning to search for wolf sign.

That night a Chinook blew in and the temperature shot up into the sixties; the snow melted, the river opened wide, and the ice never returned that year. Jerome found no wolf sign, and neither I nor anyone else has seen the wolf since that day, but I sense its presence, and I wonder at the several lambs that went missing from our flocks last spring.

* * *

8

Now, months later on this bright September day, Nodd's border seems a wonderful place to be. I daydream as I walk along the northern fence, imagining myself as a winged Seraph gliding low over hills of gold. My carbine is slung over my right shoulder, its butt slapping my butt with every other step like the hard, encouraging hand of Zerachiel. I feel safe and strong with the fence on my right and the autumn sun warming my face, hearing the faint scuff of my boots on the dry path and the rattling flight call of a meadowlark. On such a day the thought that a wolf might be raiding our flocks fills me not with fear but with reverent wonder that a creature so large, so deadly, so powerful, could make its home unseen among us.

I am thinking about this when I hear the Worldly voice.

"Hey, Cult Boy."

I jump from the path and land in a crouch, ready, my rifle pointing through the fence at . . . nothing? I look around wildly, searching for the source of the strange voice, but there is no one in sight. Did I imagine it?

"Are you gonna *shoot* me?"

He sounds young.

"Who's there?" My own words are sucked up by the sky.

"I don't want you to shoot me, Cult Boy." The voice is coming from beyond the fence.

"Don't call me that."

"Why not? You're in that cult, aren't you?"

With my ears I can tell where the voice is coming from, but my eyes see only tall grass. I move closer. Some of the grass looks different. It's not grass at all, but some sort of netting. Camouflage netting. I swing my rifle toward it.

"Show yourself," I say.

"Not with that gun pointed at me."

"I order you to show yourself."

"You got no right to order me, Cult Boy. I'm not on your land."

He is right. As long as he stays on his side of the fence, he can do whatever he wishes. We are not permitted to exert our influence beyond the borders of Nodd. I lower my gun.

"Besides," the voice says, "how do you know I don't have a gun pointed at you?" The netting rises; I can see the shape beneath it. A slim hand appears and tugs the camouflage netting aside, and I see three things:

A rifle, pointing at my belly.

A smile, lips stretched over the whitest teeth I have ever seen.

A long, unbound shock of sun-colored hair.

It is not a boy. It is a girl.

2

"My name's Lynna." The girl lowers her rifle and walks up to
the fence. She is wearing faded blue jeans, pointed boots, and
a light camouflage jacket, unzipped. Beneath the unzipped
jacket is a thin black shirt.

I step back a pace.

She laughs and shakes her head. Her long hair, the color
of autumn grass, parted in the middle, moves like a thing
alive. Her eyes are the color of the top of the sky at sunset.
Many among the Grace have blue eyes, but none so deeply
blue as hers.

"Scared of a girl?"

"You startled me," I say. "I could not see you."

"That's why it's called camouflage, Cult Boy." She gestures toward the netting with her rifle.

"Do not call me that."

"Why not? You're in that cult, aren't you?"

"We are not a *cult*."

"Yeah, right. You got a name?"

"I am Jacob Grace."

"Jake?"

"Not Jake. Jacob."

She laughs again. It makes me think of bells wrapped in velvet.

"I'm sorry I scared you, Jake-*ub*."

"I should not be speaking with you."

"How come? Am I the spawn of Satan or something? Shit."

I am struck speechless by her invoking the name of the Beast. And I have heard the word "shit" only rarely, as when Brother Wallace pronounced it after being butted by one of our rams.

"You don't talk much, do you?" she says.

I ignore her question. "What are you doing here?" I ask.

"I live here."

"I mean *here*. Right here." I point at the ground beneath her feet.

"I'm hunting," she says.

"Hunting what?"

"Cult boys." She makes her eyes go bigger, then laughs before I can say anything. "Just kidding. We lost a couple of calves out this way," she says. "Cal says there's a wolf, or a pack of 'em. We see tracks, but never the wolves." Her teeth flash in the sunlight. "Ghost wolves." I can see her neck, soft and tanned, all the way down to her collarbone. As if divining my thoughts, she shrugs off her jacket. "Getting warm out," she says.

The thin fabric of her black T-shirt does nothing to conceal the shape of her breasts. I look away. It is, in fact, warm. Beads of sweat have gathered upon my brow. I see the sheen of moisture coating her forehead as well. Vividly, and for but an instant, I imagine wiping it away with my palm.

"So tell me, O talkative one," she says. "What do you guys *do* in there all day? Just, like, pray and stuff?"

"We pray," I say. "Don't you?"

She snorts. "Yeah, right. Pray to get the hell out of Montana." She rakes her fingers through her hair, lifting it off the back of her neck.

"I should not be speaking with you." I take a step back.

Her mouth widens; her eyes become slits. Silent laughing now, like the wolf.

"It was not my intention to amuse you," I say.

"Well, you do," she says. "You're so stiff."

"I must leave." I continue walking along the fence line.

She follows me along the fence, letting her left hand drag noisily across the chain-link. "Where you going?"

"I am walking the fence line."

"You do that every day?"

I stop walking. I know I should not reveal our ways to

13

one of the World, but I hear myself say, "I walk the fence every other Landay."

"Landay?" She gives me a puzzled look.

"You call it Tuesday," I say.

"Oh. That's weird. Why don't *you* just call it Tuesday?"

"Tuesday is its pagan name." I start walking again. It bothers me that she thinks I am weird.

"See you in a couple of *Landays*," she calls after me.

I do not look back.

3

I return late to the Village.

Brother Will sees me as I trudge the last few steps to Menshome.

"Brother Jacob!" he says. "You are just now getting back?"

"I was delayed," I tell him. I have missed supper, but that is the least of my concerns. I have much to think on after my encounter with the Worldly girl.

"We gather for Babel Hour," Will says. "Hurry!"

I have forgotten. Tonight the unmarried men and women of Nodd gather in the Hall of Enoch for Singles Services, better known as Babel Hour, the most eagerly anticipated event of the week, for it is the only time we men are encouraged to speak to the unmarried Sisters, and they to us. And there will be food.

For the moment, thoughts of the Worldly girl are driven from my head. I cleanse my hands, face, and feet, change into my formal garb, and make my way to the Hall of Enoch.

Babel Hour starts with we unwed Brothers, thirteen in number, standing at one side of the hall. We are wearing our robes of somber gray, the color of fortitude. The eight unwed Sisters, gowned and scarved in pale, modest earthen tones, line the opposite wall. Elder Abraham Grace enters the room, takes his place behind the pulpit, and leads us in callbacks. Elder Abraham has four score and six years, but his voice still rolls with Heaven's thunder.

"And Arphaxad lived five and thirty years—" he booms, facing the women.

The women do not respond immediately. That first call comes out of nowhere, and it is often hard to know which Scripture he is quoting.

"And begat Salah," one of the women calls back. It's Sister Olivia Grace, one of the older unmarried women.

Abraham turns to the men. *"And Arphaxad lived after he begat Salah four hundred and three years—"* says Elder Abraham.

"And begat sons and daughters," shout several of the men. It's easier once you find your place. Tonight, Abraham has chosen Genesis, which we know well.

"And Salah lived thirty years—" Abraham calls to the women.

"And begat Eber," shout nearly all of the women with one voice.

We're rolling now. It goes, back and forth, the men competing with the women to recall every line.

Elder Abraham can keep it up for more than an hour before his voice gives out, but on this night he ends with Genesis 11—*and Terah died in Haran.* It is time for snacks and conversation. That's the good part.

And the part that scares me.

Sister Ruth, daughter of Peter and Naomi, has eyes the color of honey, with flecks of green. Like all the Sisters, Ruth keeps her hair tied back in a bun and covered with a scarf, but her hair is so thick and willful that no matter how tightly she binds it, a few coils of brown always manage to escape. I think about her hair a lot, the fingers of my mind gently tucking those loose strands back beneath her scarf. During Babel Hour, my eyes constantly seek her out. Tonight she is at the far end of the row of women, shouting out responses confidently, a faint smile playing across her lips as she waits for the next call.

She is radiant; the Lord has filled her with light.

Once, I see her turn in my direction. I think it is me she's looking at, or so I hope, as I plan to marry Sister Ruth. I have known since we were small children that she would be my wife. When I think of the future, of the years of waiting for the angel Zerachiel to come for us, I think of Ruth and me together. It has always been thus.

In less than a year, I will come of age. I will go to Father Grace and I will ask him to give her unto me. I cannot imagine him refusing.

Again, her eyes seek me out, and I hold her gaze for a moment before looking away. An image of the Worldly girl flashes before my eyes; I push it away. The Worldly girl has no place here.

Elder Abraham voices a short benediction, then invites the women to display their offerings. From within their robes, the women produce packets of sweets and savories. They unwrap them and lay them out on the long trestle table at the end of the room as we men watch and wonder at other treasures hidden beneath their modest garb. Once the treats are laid out, the women return to their places, and we men are permitted to examine and sample their offerings.

Father Grace's son, Von, with his shorn scalp and doughy features, is the first to the table. He snatches several treats, shoving them into the sleeves of his robe, then quickly retreats to the far side of the hall, where he fits himself into the corner and begins to eat. Everyone ignores him. Von is not right in the head, but he is harmless.

The rest of us gather before the trestle table and admire our Sisters' work.

Sister Ruth Grace has prepared a selection of small crescent-shaped savories decorated with seeds: some with nigella, some with amaranth, some with poppy. I take a plate and select one of each, along with several of the other women's treats. I have not eaten in many hours, and my body is shaky from the long walk.

There is more to do than eat. Under the vigilant eye of Elder Abraham, as we sample each of the treats we have selected, we engage the women in conversation.

"Who among you prepared this chocolate drop cookie?" asks Brother John Grace. Brother John, at twenty-nine, is one of the eldest of the unmarried men. With his exceptionally long nose and spotted complexion, he is also among the least well-favored.

"It was I," says Sister Beryl.

"It is sublime."

"Th-thank you, Brother John." Sister Beryl's cheeks flush red. Beryl is a slight girl with a wan, frightened expression. She has just turned fourteen. This is her first Babel Hour.

I bite into Sister Ruth's poppy seed crescent. It is savory, moist, and still warm with the heat of her body.

"This is an excellent cruller!" exclaims Brother Will Grace.

"Thank you, Brother Will," says Sister Angela. "I had hoped you would enjoy it."

Brother Will nods seriously and pushes the rest of the cruller into his wide mouth. Will is known for his appetite, though he is thin as a broom handle.

I gird myself to offer my compliments to Sister Ruth, but Brother Benedict speaks first.

"The amaranth crescent is a wonder," he says, smiling at her. "Do I detect a hint of nutmeg?"

"You do indeed," says Sister Ruth.

"The poppy seed crescent is most perfect," I blurt out.

"G'bless, Brother Jacob," says Sister Ruth, even as Brother Benedict frowns upon me.

I feel my face turning red. It is considered rude to direct two compliments in a row to the same woman, and I have both embarrassed myself and incurred Brother Benedict's ill favor. This is no small matter, as Benedict, who trained for seven years in a Worldly college, teaches us our letters and the history of the World.

The other men declare their appreciations. The conversation begins to loosen and become more personal. Brother Luke asks after the health of Sister Angela's mother, who is suffering from shingles. Sister Mara, one of the boldest of the women, asks Brother Gregory to sample her lavender biscuits. I try to speak again to Ruth, but Brother Jerome is between us, telling her that the amaranth crop is coming in strong. I bite into a honey cake made by Sister Louise. It is too sweet and dry, and I have trouble swallowing. Sister Louise sees me replace the remains of the tiny cake on my plate. I want to reassure her, to lie to her, but my mouth is full of dry sweet cake and all I can do is smile and nod. She quickly looks away. I devour another of Ruth's crescents to wash away the sour honey taste. Once again I attempt to approach Ruth, but now she is talking with Brother Luke. For a brief instant, her eyes slip past him and we are looking at each other. She smiles, and I am certain her smile is for me.

Elder Abraham claps his hands three times. His hands are large enough to cover a dinner plate; the claps ring out like gunshots.

We men return our plates to the table and line up against the wall opposite the women. There is a vibration in the room, a barely suppressed excitement from both sides. Were it not for the kind strictures placed upon us by Father Grace and Zerachiel the Lord's Command, we might become no more than animals, swept away by tides of lust.

Elder Abraham's voice fills the room: "'And the Lord said unto Abraham, Yea, I know that thou didst this in the integrity of thy heart; for I also withheld thee from sinning against me: therefore suffered I thee not to touch her. Now therefore restore the man his wife; for he is a prophet, and he shall pray for thee, and thou shalt live: and if thou restore her not, know thou that thou shalt surely die, thou, and all that are thine.'"

Babel Hour is come to a close.

The women leave the hall first. Elder Abraham leads the men in a prayer of cleansing and digestion, after which we are allowed to retire to Menshome. I am walking with Brother Will, taking the longer route around the Sacred Heart. My traitorous thoughts have returned to the Worldly girl, and I feel an urge to share with Will what happened, but as I open my mouth to confess to him, I notice, on the grassy verge beside the crushed-rock path ahead of us, a scrap of pale cloth. I am about to remark upon it to Brother Will when a door bangs open. A figure dashes out from Womenshome onto the verge and snatches up the scrap of cloth. She is barefooted, and her long dark hair is loose and free about her shoulders. Seeing the two of us, she lets out a squeak of alarm, then runs quickly back inside. As the door slams, we hear an explosion of high-pitched giggling.

Brother Will and I stop and look at each other in shock.

"Was that not Sister Ruth?" Brother Will says.

"It was," I say, as my phallus swells with the black blood of desire.

I say nothing to Will or anyone else of my encounter with the Worldly girl, and it may be too late. If I go to Brother Enos now, he will chastise me first for interrupting him at his evening prayers, and then again for not going to him immediately upon my return from my patrol. And what could I say? That I was late because I had paused to chat with a Worldly rifle-toting girl? That I had not come to him directly because I did not wish to miss Babel Hour? That after Babel Hour, I had been so consumed with lustful thoughts of both Sister Ruth and the Worldly girl that I came first here, to Sinners' Chapel, to purify myself with a cedar switch?

I grit my teeth and strike three more blows.

The red cedar that grows on the hillsides produces large numbers of small, sharp needles. To brush up against one is slightly unpleasant, but to slap a needled branch hard against one's naked flesh is a blow from the hand of Zerachiel. Shirtless, I flail my back until the stinging becomes burning, the burning an exquisite throbbing, the throbbing a soul-searing agony. I do not stop until that which lies below my waist feels as far away and insignificant as the faintest star in the blackest sky.

By the time I place the branch in the brazier, offering up a final prayer for absolution, I have hardly enough life in me to stagger through the dark night to Menshome. On this day I have walked thirteen miles and beaten myself well and good. Still, it is nothing compared to the punishment I might yet receive from Brother Enos should he fathom my transgressions.

Brother Will and Brother Gregory are reading Scripture in the common room, sitting shoulder to shoulder beneath the single bulb. I walk past them without speaking. They look up, but do not remark upon the dark streaks on the back of my robe. I retire to my cell, strip naked, and curl up on my mattress of straw ticking, lying on my side to keep my weeping back from gluing itself to the rough sheets.

I pray for sleep, but I am charged with memories. How badly have I sinned? And was my sin of speaking with the Worldly girl lesser or greater than the sin of not telling Brother Enos of my indiscretion?

My back burns with the fire of penitence. Can I yet redeem myself by confessing? Or have my sins hurled me beyond the boundaries of redemption? Even now, as I lie curled in this sickle of pain, images of Sister Ruth and the Worldly girl Lynna dance about the tattered edges of my soul. Brother Will is snoring in the next cell. I envy him his deep sleep, and wonder how he can rest so easily after laying eyes upon Sister Ruth, bareheaded and barefooted. Ruth's dark tresses tangle in my head with Lynna's golden crown, and once again the Beast attacks me through my groin.

4

I rise early so that I may perform my morning ablutions alone. I wash, dress, and take myself to the Sacred Heart. The sun is yet unrisen, but Brother Andrew is already on his ancient knees in his flower beds, planting new bulbs, preparing the gardens for the long winter that is to come, his long white beard soiled from dragging in the fresh-turned earth. Andrew has been frenzied in recent weeks, ministering to his plantings as if every hour might be his last, as well it might, given his great age.

In the Village, every space not covered by a building or a pathway is devoted to our gardens. Under Brother Andrew's care, the flowers come up more beautiful and profuse with every spring. One day our gardens of Nodd will rival those of the first Eden, and the Tree will bear sweet fruit, and the Ark will come.

I kneel at the wall and pray, but I cannot bring myself to pray for Zerachiel's coming. Not yet. As the words of the Arbor Prayer pass over my tongue, I am thinking of Ruth. I am thinking of Lynna. I pray with my lips as I sin in my heart.

When the sun rises, I break my fast in the dining room in Menshome. Will is already shoveling down a stew of broad beans and potatoes. We will need full bellies, for on this day we will be many hours in the fields.

My father, Elder Nathan, comes in and asks if any of us know where he can find Brother Taylor.

"He took the Jeep into West Fork," John says. "He said he had to pick up a part for the tractor." Brother Taylor maintains our vehicles and mechanical equipment. He is one of the few Grace who deal regularly with the World.

"Ask him to see Sister Elena when he returns," my father says. Sister Elena is my mother. "She is having trouble with one of the washing machines."

I feel his eyes pass over me. I fear that he can see into my stained and sullied heart. To avoid his eyes, I bend my head over my plate and fill myself with hot stew.

My father heard the call of Father Grace when I was yet a child. Back then he was known as Nate Green. He was a lawyer in Omaha, Nebraska, but he was not a happy man. The vacuum of the World had emptied his soul, and it was not until he met Father Grace that he began to find himself again.

My mother opened her heart to Father Grace as well, and

shortly thereafter my parents gave unto him all their Worldly possessions and took themselves here to Nodd.

I remember that first life vaguely, like a faraway dream. I remember television, and our dog, Spots, and a boy named Bobby who lived next door. I remember playing on a swing, and a few other things. Or maybe I remember only because my mother has told me of these things. I had but five summers when we came to Nodd.

My father does not often speak of the past, although once, as a way of explaining my failure at some small task, he told me that I had been conceived in sin. I remember it as if it had happened yesterday. In a moment of anger, he told me that his next child would be pure and clean as January snow.

Later that same day, my mother came to me as I was cleaning the chicken coops. She put her arm around me and said, "You were conceived in love, Jacob. The fact that your father and I were not married at the time cannot change that."

"Are you saying he is wrong?"

"Your father is a man, Jacob. He is a good man, but he has much anger inside him, and sometimes it spills over onto those he loves."

"He told me you would bear him a pure boy."

My mother laughed and shook her head so hard a strand of hair fell across her face. She tucked it back, looked around to see if anyone was watching, then quickly kissed me on my forehead.

"You are pure enough for me," she said, and left me with the chickens.

That was years ago. Because it is the will of the Lord, the fruit of my mother's womb has failed to set, and I remain my father's only — his tainted — issue.

My mother is not best loved amongst the Grace, for she has a way of speaking her mind when she should not, she is reluctant to give praise where she perceives mediocrity, and she speaks often of Worldly things. My mother is as devout as any, but she will at times say things like, "What wouldn't I give for a double cappuccino right now!" Or she will say of Elder Seth, who is known for his inflexibility and sour demeanor, "Someone should tell that man to move his bowels."

But she has a softer side, and during those odd times when we find ourselves together for a moment, as when she delivers laundry to Menshome, she tells me things of her early life, and of the World.

Brother Will and I are assigned by Brother Peter to follow the scythe wielders and gather the cornstalks. We Grace plant but a few acres of corn. Wheat and rye, our staple grains, have already been gathered. The corn harvest takes but a single day, then on to the lentils, the beans, the squashes, the root vegetables.

Brothers Jerome and Aaron swing their scythes in great, forceful arcs, slicing through the thick cornstalks inches above the dry Montana soil, sending up billows of dust and chaff. Jerome looks back, sees how closely I follow, and swings his scythe low, scuffing the powdery earth, raising a cloud so thick I stop and hold my sleeve over my mouth and nose. Jerome laughs.

Our job is to gather sheaves of cornstalks and tie them loosely together into hattocks. Behind us, the shorn field is studded with such rough teepees. I slow my pace to let the reapers get farther ahead, and to let Will catch up. Will works slowly, as always. His sluggishness can be irritating at times. I build three hattocks to his two.

If the weather holds true and clear over the next three weeks, the ears of corn will dry, after which we will strip them from their stalks and haul them on wagons to the granary. There the ears will finish drying in mesh silos. Come November, the kernels will be twisted from the cobs to be ground into coarse meal for quick bread and sweet porridge.

I recognize my mother, one of three Sisters who follow us down the rows of corn, gleaning stray ears that have fallen from the stalks, loading them into cloth sacks they wear on their backs. My mother gleans with the speed of a hungry goose. As she bends and plucks ears of corn from where they have fallen, she sings under her breath. I hear a wisp of melody, an old song that I remember her singing to me as a young child. There is little singing among us, as music leads to temptations of the flesh, but in the fields, with the Elders out of earshot, my mother sings. It is not long before she comes close enough to speak with me.

"Jacob," she says, "you perform the work of three. Slow yourself, lest you leave poor William feeling unworthy."

"If Will feels unworthy he should move more quickly," I say, then regret my remark and look around to be sure that Will is not close enough to have overheard.

"I fear you have inherited my own intemperance," she says.

"Apologies, Sister. I did not sleep soundly."

"I hear your voice rings strong at Babel Hour."

I feel my face redden. This causes my mother to laugh out loud.

"That your loins whisper to you is no cause for shame."

"I am not ashamed," I say, although I am far more ashamed than she could know.

"If I may guess, is it Sister Ruth who catches thine eye?" she says.

I cannot lie aloud to my mother twice, so I look down at the fresh-cut corn stubble and nod.

"I pray there are others you look favorably upon as well," she says.

I look up sharply. This is a very strange thing for her to say. For a moment I fear she knows of the Worldly girl, but the concern I behold upon my mother's sun-browned features shows no hint of censure. It is something else.

"Brother!" It is Brother Jerome, looking back, telling me with his frown that I am not doing my part.

"G'bless, Sister," I say to my mother, and return to my work.

We are blessed with a stretch of dry days that are perfect for the harvest. Brother Peter works us hard and long, and I do not think overmuch of Sister Ruth or the Worldly girl. By Manday much of the work is behind us. We trudge in from the fields, looking forward to a hot meal, early to bed, and to waking on Sabbathday, our day of rest. But when we enter the Village I see a black SUV parked before the Hall of Enoch.

All thoughts of food and sleep fly from my head.

Father Grace has returned to Nodd.

2

And his face was dazzling and
glorious and terrible to behold.
—Enoch 89:23

5

For the past six weeks, Father Grace and his wives have been tending the Grace Ministries in Colorado Springs and Omaha, so that others might hear him and join us in Nodd. But few are willing to give up all their Worldly possessions. Father Grace has been preaching the words of Zerachiel for thirty years now, yet only we three score and two have embraced the truth of his calling.

Still, at times he returns from his journeys with converts, and we welcome them. There is always great excitement when new Grace enter our lives. On this occasion, a rumor passes through the Menshome like the wind: Father Grace has brought with him four new souls.

* * *

The Convocation to celebrate Father Grace's return is to begin immediately after supper. I wash with the other men, too hurried to keep my scabbed back safe from their eyes. Brother Will notices, but he makes no comment. We are all sinners. As we dry ourselves and don our meeting robes, the bells calling us to Convocation begin to toll.

The Hall of Enoch is large enough to hold thrice our number, and one day it may well do so. We gather, all of us, from Sister Mary's youngest, born in August, to Sister Agatha, mother to Enos, small and bent hard over her walker. We are one, crowded at the front of the hall, as Father Grace enters and mounts the platform, followed by his entourage.

Father Grace is a large man, standing a hand above four cubits. His black beard, shot with streaks of gray, spills over his vast trunk. Long gray hair falls straight and thick to his broad shoulders. His right eye, black as his beard, scours our faces. The left eye, pale gray nested in a whorl of scar tissue, gazes upon Heaven, blind to this World of dust and dross.

The Archcherubim Enos and Caleb take their places to either side of him. Father Grace's three wives arrange themselves to Enos's left, sitting with their hands folded in their laps, smiling over us with alert, self-satisfied smiles.

It is said that Father Grace has eighty years, though my mother once told me that he is only a few years older than my father, who is fifty-eight. Whatever his true age, Father Grace's vigor is vast. As he takes his place behind the pulpit and raises his long arms, one can imagine that he could gather all of us together in one mighty embrace.

And so he stands silent before us, as is his custom, arms thrust out, his glittering black eye raking across us, seeing into our stained and spattered souls. I stare straight ahead, imagining with all my might the angel Zerachiel astride his steed of ivory. I wish I had beaten myself harder.

Father Grace holds knowledge beyond the ken of ordinary men. He has been known to foretell a Grace's sins, and to offer penance for deeds as yet undone. Once, as he was striding past the prayer wall surrounding the Tree, he stopped suddenly and pulled Sister Mara from the wall and struck her a great blow. I heard this from Brother John, who was present at the time.

"Father," she cried, "what have I done?"

"It is what you would have done," said Father Grace. He then embraced her and forgave her for her uncommitted sin. Later, Sister Mara confessed to lusting after a man who had been seduced by the World and who had left Nodd some months earlier. Father Grace's actions had prevented her from following the apostate and dooming her soul to an eternity in Hell.

The Convocation is dead silent, without so much as a rustle of cloth, when Father Grace opens his mouth to speak.

"Brethren," he says, "it is the Lord's day." Father Grace's voice is not the voice one might expect from a man so imposing and hirsute. It is as light as beaten cream. With closed eyes, one might almost imagine him to be a woman. Nevertheless, his utterances possess the force of thunder. We listen as he relates the story of Moses in the desert and of the prophets

Enoch, Jesus, and Joseph. He follows this with his own tale of redemption, of his struggles as a young man to find his Faith. It is a tale he tells often, and of which we never tire.

As the familiar words roll across us, I let my eyes stray to the women's side of the temple, searching for Sister Ruth's dark curls, but I cannot pick her out from the mass of identical clay-colored headscarves. I force my attention back to Father Grace.

"And though I had but twenty years, I had tasted all the false religions of the World and found them wanting: Catholics worshipping both graven images and the pope, who is in truth the Antichrist; Lutherans, Baptists, all wallowing in the glorification of their tarnished selves; Jews with hearts of avarice and greed; pagans writhing, painted and naked, at their unholy rites; Muslims eating their children and bowing to the false god Mohammad. Even the Latter-day Saints, who raised me, twisted the Words of the Almighty to suit their mercenary agenda. I was lost, searching the faithless wilderness for the Truth. I rode upon my motorcycle from church to church, from one false prophet to the next, and found my hopes dashed again and again. I even sought wisdom from the American savages. It was then that the Lord struck me down.

"It happened on a Monday, what we now call Heavenday. I had been riding all night toward the land of the Hopi, my mind clouded with false tales of ancient wisdom. I still had hope, even after my many disappointments. The sun had yet to rise; the mesas were a dark slash against the slate-gray sky; the wind tore like eagles' talons at my face, and it was then that the Lord sent Zerachiel to smite me, first in the guise of a white coyote in the road before me. I swerved to avoid the beast. The tires of my motorcycle lost purchase. I flew through the air and landed hard in the ditch, where I lay stunned amidst the scraps of shredded truck tires, beer cans, and plastic shopping bags fluttering in the wind.

"The heavens opened. Raindrops the size of cherries pelted my body. I rose to my feet, bruised and in pain but without serious injury. My motorcycle had not fared so well. As I stared down at the twisted metal, the raindrops hardened to become hail. I looked around, seeking shelter. There were no buildings, no trees, only patches of brush and cactus. I saw a rocky outcropping a few hundred cubits away. With no promise of shelter elsewhere, I ran for the rocks. By the time I reached them, I was being beaten by hailstones the size of walnuts. The rocks provided partial shelter. I was able to squeeze beneath a shallow overhang to wait out the storm.

"I had been there for but moments when the Lord struck. The rock exploded. Lightning lanced through my eye and into my soul. I was thrown from my rude shelter and landed upon my back.

"There is much I do not remember of that night. In the morning, I awakened in agony, unable to move, the desert sun piercing my flesh. For three days and nights, I lay on my back staring up into the heavens, my blasted eye throbbing with the sublime torment of seeing Heaven in all its plenteous and unstinting glory, even as my untouched eye wept with sorrow for all the sinners, not least of all myself. And as I lay there in misery, with scorpions crawling over my body and the sun cracking my skin and vultures circling high above, I was visited by an angel whose features were too bright to look upon, and he named himself Zerachiel, and he told me I was to bear a message of salvation.

"'I cannot,' I said. 'I am dying.'

"'You will not die,' Zerachiel said. 'You have work to do.'

"But even with this promise, my body would not obey me. 'Why me?' I cried out."

Father Grace pauses, as he always does at that point, with upthrust arms, both eyes seeking Heaven. Slowly his arms drop to his sides and his chin comes down until his black eye once again falls upon us.

"And Zerachiel, whose face was brighter than the sun, looked down upon me and said, 'The Holy Scriptures contain much truth, but that truth is veiled. The Lord has chosen you to lift that veil.'"

Father Grace stares down at us from the pulpit.

"As he has chosen each and every one of us. And today we rejoice, for the Lord has brought us four new souls." He holds his hands out toward the front of the room, and a moment later, three figures climb onto the platform to stand before him: an older woman, a younger woman heavy with child, and a boy of perhaps fifteen summers. They have not yet donned the garb of the Grace. The older woman is wearing a long black skirt and a green sweater. Her graying hair hangs unbound on either side of her face. She is smiling but clearly nervous. The younger woman has on stretchy blue jeans so tight I can see the bulge of her thighs. Her belly, swollen with child, presses out against a loose short-sleeved blouse. She looks tired.

The boy is also wearing jeans, but his are loose and puddled over his athletic shoes. Printed in orange upon his blue hooded sweatshirt is the word BRONCOS. He has short reddish-blond hair and freckles. His small eyes dart from face to face until they land upon me, and a flat smile creeps across the boy's broad cheeks.

6

The boy is called Tobias. He is from a town called Limon, in Colorado. Brother Enos has charged me with helping him to learn our ways.

"This will be your cell," I tell him, showing him where he will sleep.

"Cell." He wrinkles his stubby nose at the pallet. "Great."

I pull open the wide drawer beneath the pallet. "For your garments. Brother John will provide you with four changes of clothing. Two for work, one for meetings, and one for daily wear."

Tobias looks me up and down. "Which is *that*?"

"This is my meeting robe. It is made of wool from our sheep."

"It looks like a dress. You look like a long-haired, fuzzy-faced girl," he says.

"It is comfortable and clean," I tell him.

"It's the color of mud."

"Vanity is a sin."

He rolls his eyes. "I'll wear my own clothes, thanks. Wool makes me itch. Besides, this place could use a little color."

I doubt that he will be permitted this conceit for long, but I say nothing.

He says, "And what's with all the hair?"

"What do you mean?"

"Doesn't anybody ever get a haircut? Or shave?"

"It is not our way." I wonder if I am being tested.

"What about that bald-headed dude? What's his deal?"

"That is Brother Von. He is . . . special."

"Yeah, he *looks* special."

"You must turn your mattress every morning," I say. I do not want to talk about Von.

"Yeah, yeah." He looks around the cell. "I've been in bigger closets. And what's with the no door? You don't believe in doors?"

"Why would you want a door?" I ask.

He shakes his head, looking at me as if I am a mindless fool. He is so disdainful. I want to impress him, to show him something that will strike him deep and hard. My first thought is to take him into the Sacred Heart, to show him the Tree. But I am loath to show this Worldly boy our most sacred place, at least not right away, so I suggest we take a walk up the Spine.

"Spine?"

"That which separates the Meadows from the Mire."

"What's on this *spine*?"

"You will see. We will go in the morning."

"Whatever," he says with a shrug.

I awaken Tobias near the close of the morning meal service. He is not happy. He thrashes aside his covers. He has slept in his clothes. He mutters something about it being still dark out.

"The sun is rising," I say. "It will be full light by the time you finish eating."

"I'm not hungry," he says.

"We have a long walk. You should eat."

Grumbling, he follows me to the dining area. We have the tables to ourselves. Everyone else has already eaten and gone about their tasks. I show him how to serve himself. This morning, we have oatmeal, bread, and apples. There were egg cakes earlier, but they have been eaten. He wrinkles his nose at the oatmeal, but he loads his plate with slices of bread and several spoonfuls of huckleberry preserves. I make no comment.

"Aren't you eating?" he asks me.

"I have eaten," I say.

He grunts, bites into a slice of bread, chews, scowls.

"Sour," he says. "Don't you have any regular bread?"

"This is our bread."

44

He eats the rest of his slice, then half of another, and declares himself done. I show him what to do with his plate. I wrap his uneaten bread in waxed paper and hand it to him.

"You may want it later," I say.

"I doubt it." But he takes the packet and shoves it into the belly pocket of his sweatshirt.

"Are you ready?" I ask.

He nods glumly and follows me out of Menshome.

I turn up the pathway leading west, toward the Spine. Tobias follows me for a few paces, then stops, looking up at the Tower, which stands behind Elderlodge.

"Weird-looking silo," he says. "I never seen one made out of rock."

"It is not a silo. It is the Tower."

"What's it for?"

"It is a lookout." The Tower, made of stone blocks cut from the walls of the Pison gorge, stands thirty cubits tall.

"Lookout for what?"

"Whatever may come."

"Weird." He turns a slow circle, surveying our surroundings: the Tower, Elderlodge, Menshome, and the tall hedge enclosing the Sacred Heart. "It's kind of like a little pretend town."

"There is no pretending here."

He makes a sound that is half laugh, half snort.

Irritated, I start walking up the pathway without looking

back. After a dozen or so long paces. I hear him run to catch up. He may not be impressed by our dress, our food, our grooming, or our buildings, but it is my hope he will be roused by what lies at the head of the Spine.

On the north side of the Low Meadows, the land rises steeply to form a twisting ridge that separates the Meadows from the cedar bog we call the Mire. The Mire is the least favored of our lands, good for collecting mushrooms and medicinal mosses but little else. The Spine itself is a tree-studded, rocky hump that snakes to the west for more than a mile, climbing slowly, then ending abruptly at the Pison River. From the rocky out-cropping high above the gorge, the place we call the Knob, one can see, on a clear day, the teeth of the western mountains nibbling the horizon.

But this day is not clear. The sky is low and gray; a chill wind cuts through the loose weave of my woolen tunic and my cotton shirt as we follow the trail west. Tobias puts up his hood and tucks his hands in the front pocket of his thick sweatshirt. I pretend not to let the cold bother me, though a part of me envies him his heavy, colorful garment.

We reach the Meadows and turn north. The land slowly rises. As we walk, I tell him of our sheep, our milk cows, and the harvest. "There is much to do here," I say. "The fences always need mending, the animals need care, the crops need tending."

"At least you don't have to go to school."

"Brother Benedict and others school us in the winter, when there is less to do. We are very well educated. I have learned writing, and numbers, and the geography and peoples of the World, and the Holy Scriptures."

"You're a regular Einstein," Tobias says.

"What is 'Einstein'?" I ask.

He snorts. His scorn is palpable; I feel myself growing angry, but I press on.

"The Cherubim are granted many interesting tasks."

"What is 'Cherubim'?" he asks.

"All men of thirteen years, if they are pure of heart and willing to work, become Cherubim and move to Menshome with the other unmarried men. Before that, we live in Elderlodge with our parents."

"So at thirteen your folks kicked you out?"

"There was no kicking. It is an honor to be a Cherub."

"What about the girls?"

"It is the same. At thirteen, they leave Elderlodge and go to live in Womenshome until they are wed. At eighteen, men who have applied themselves become Higher Cherubim. They have the right to audit the Council of Elders, and to take a wife. Higher Cherubim who distinguish themselves might one day join the Archcherubim."

"One-Eye—I suppose he's one of them."

I stop walking and turn to him. "One-Eye?"

"You know. Father Grace."

"Father Grace has *two* eyes."

"Yeah, but one's all goofy."

"His blasted eye remains fixed upon the Heavens, waiting for Zerachiel."

"In Colorado Springs, he wore a patch."

I am not surprised; Father Grace covers his blasted eye when he leaves Nodd.

"Father Grace is first amongst the Elders. He lives in Gracehome, behind Elderlodge."

Tobias snorts. "You guys got weird names for everything, don't you? What do you call the toilets?"

"The toilets," I say.

"You really believe all that stuff about the Apocalypse and all?"

"It is the Truth."

"Yeah, right. The thing is, the world was supposed to end in 2012, according to the Mayans. Only here we are."

"The Mayans are Lamanite heathens. The Apocalypse is foretold in the Scriptures."

He gives me a doubtful look. "Whatever."

We continue our slow climb. Neither of us speaks for a time. I push aside my irritation at his contemptuous attitude. It is not Tobias's fault that he is ignorant. His soul is stained by a life of garish colors and Worldly vice. I think of Lynna and once again feel the sting of the cedar switch upon my back. It itches now, a reminder of my own sins.

Tobias, at least, has ignorance as an excuse.

The way steepens. The sun finds a rent in the clouds and

warms my side. Soon we are both perspiring; Tobias pushes his hood back and unzips the front of his sweatshirt.

"I thought you said it wasn't far," he says. We have been walking for a scant twenty minutes and have yet to reach the trees.

"It will be worth it," I say.

He grunts in response. We follow a twisting path up a boulder-strewn hillside, and then we are in the trees and everything changes. The foliage filters the sound of the wind, replacing it with the soft, grainy murmur of the high forest. We follow the needle-carpeted path deeper into the trees. Tobias is several strides behind me, but I can hear him breathing. I stop and turn toward him.

"What?" he says, trying to cover up the fact that he is out of breath.

"Do you want to rest?"

"I'm okay." He looks around. The reddish trunks of the pines rise like the pillars of Heaven. I hear the croak of a raven and the vexed chatter of a pine squirrel. "These trees are, like, *huge,*" he says.

"They are ponderosa pines."

"I saw redwoods once, in California, with my dad. They get twice that big."

I find it difficult to credit his claim, but I do not wish to argue.

"How much farther?" he asks.

"Not far."

The path along the crest of the Spine is tortuous and

uneven, but well trodden and easy to follow. I notice Tobias falling behind again, so I stop and wait for him to catch up. He is panting, not even trying to hide it.

"It's the altitude," I say as we move slowly up the path. "You will become accustomed to it, Lord willing."

"Yeah, well, the Lord can relax on account of I don't expect to stick around here that long," he says.

"Where are you going?"

"Costa Rica."

I know that Costa Rica is a tiny country in Central America. Brother Benedict has drilled us well in the geography of the World. But I cannot imagine going there, for it seems as unreal and distant as the moon.

"My dad lives there. With his girlfriend."

"Girlfriend!" I say. The concept is both thrilling and disturbing.

"I had a girlfriend," Tobias says. "Back in Limon. Only we broke up."

Much as I want to hear more about his girlfriend, I say nothing and start walking again.

"What about you?" he asks. "Do you have a girl?"

"Yes," I say. "Sister Ruth. We will marry soon."

"Ruth. Is she the skinny one with the long nose and the zits?"

"No!" He is describing Rebecca.

Tobias laughs. "I was kidding. I bet I know which one's Ruth. The one with green eyes, right?"

"They are the color of honey, with green flecks."

"Yeah, I know who you mean. I was looking at her when we were up on that stage last night. She's hot!" He laughs again. "I mean, she has a cute face—I don't know what else she's got under all that stuff they wear. For all I know, she's got three boobs or something. . . . Hey, what's the matter?"

I have stopped walking. I turn on him. "You will not speak of her that way." My voice is tight, and my face is hot.

"What way? I just—" He steps back and holds up his hands. "Whoa, take it easy!"

The fear in his face stops me. I loosen my fists. Was I about to strike him?

"I *get* it," he says. "Ruth is your girl. I *get* it! Jeez! I was *kidding*!"

Suddenly I am embarrassed. I turn away and start walking quickly. Tobias runs to catch up with me.

"Wait up! I'm sorry!"

I do not trust myself to speak.

"Look, back in Limon—"

"We are not *in* Limon."

"I'm just saying, back in Limon, all the guys kid around a lot. The girls don't mind. I didn't mean anything by it."

"You should not say what you do not mean."

I walk faster, almost running. Behind me I hear him muttering his Worldly curses. Soon, he is far behind me, and for a time I walk in peace. My thoughts go to Ruth, and then, oddly, to Lynna. I stop and wait. Tobias catches up, panting.

"I know another girl, too," I say. "A Worldly girl." I don't understand why I am telling him this, but it comes out of me. "She lives on the ranch to the north. Her name is Lynna."

"So you have two girlfriends?" He laughs. "I guess it makes sense, what with Father Grace being married to three women."

"That is not what this is," I say, startled by his suggestion. "I just know her—that's all."

"Is she cute?"

I see Lynna's face in my mind.

"She is very beautiful," I say.

"Maybe the three of us could hang out sometime," he says.

"I don't know her that well." I wish I hadn't mentioned her.

The path takes a sharp turn to the right, then climbs a hillock. We are close.

Tobias says, "What's that noise?"

"You will see," I say.

The trees become smaller and more sparse, and the carpet of needles gives way to bare rock. We leave the last of the trees behind to face an enormous outcropping of gray stone: a boulder more than thirty cubits across, its sides mottled with lichen and moss, its top scrubbed smooth by the wind.

The sound is much louder now. I scramble up the side of the massive boulder and stand on top, leaning slightly into the wind. Tobias joins me. Together we look down into the gorge. He gasps.

*　*　*

52

It is said that there are men and women who believe the Almighty does not exist. I would bring them here, to this place. From the Knob, one can look straight down past layer after layer of ancient rock to the roiling, rocky silver ribbon that is the Pison. Here the hand of the Lord sliced through stone like a knife through ripened cheese, tearing a slot for the river to pass through the ridge. Below us, the Pison bellows and thunders, using the walls of the chasm as its megaphone. Who could stand here and deny the magnificence and truth and power of the Lord?

Tobias is struck nearly, though not entirely, speechless.

He says, "Holy shit."

7

There is a thing I do that frightens me, but I cannot resist. I move closer to the edge, to where the rock curves sharply down, to where the slightest urge might send me tumbling down the sheer stone face, and I imagine my last moments. I think that if I were pure, if I were not soiled by a lifetime of sin, Zerachiel would catch me in his palm and place me gently and unharmed upon this earth. I lean out over the precipice and look down at the Pison and feel the pulse of the heavens beating against my chest.

Brother Caleb, who teaches us our numbers, once told me that the rapids lie more than two hundred cubits below the Knob. He counted it by throwing a stone and measuring how long it took for the rock to strike bottom. I have tried to repeat his experiment many times since, counting down the seconds, but never yet have I been able to see the stone strike that tumbling, foaming surface. Brother Caleb must have the eyes of an eagle.

"Hey! What are you doing?"

I look back at Tobias. He is standing well back from the edge, his broad face so pale that freckles stand out like scattered embers.

"I will not fall," I tell him.

"I thought you were gonna *jump!*"

"I will not jump." I back away from the abyss to make him more comfortable.

Tobias shakes his head as color returns to his face. "You're crazy, you know that?" He slide steps toward the gorge, legs bent, looks over the edge, then backs away quickly. "It must be, like, a mile deep."

He reaches into his pocket and pulls out a red-and-white paper packet. I think it is candy at first, but he shakes out a short white tube with a brown tip. I recognize it as a cigarette.

Tobacco use is not unknown among the Grace. We cultivate a small strip of the weed along the north edge of the vegetable gardens. Most of our tobacco crop is steeped in water for use as a pesticide, but a few of the older Brothers dry a portion of the harvest and smoke it in pipes. Brothers Jerome and John mix the leaves with sorghum syrup and chew them while they work in the fields. I tried it once, but my stomach rebelled, much to Jerome's amusement.

While tobacco use is not strictly forbidden, it is frowned

upon for younger Grace such as myself. I am shocked to see Tobias set fire to the cigarette with a plastic lighter. He draws the smoke deep into his lungs.

"I'd offer you one," he says, "but I only got half a pack. I got a feeling cigs are hard to come by around here."

"You would have to go to West Fork," I say.

"How far is that?"

"About twenty-five miles. I have been there. Once."

"How long have you lived here?"

"Almost twelve years."

"And you've only been to town *once*?"

"Yes. To take a test."

"What sort of test?"

"Numbers, history, reading, and such. The Worldly powers demanded that we demonstrate the efficacy of our education. We performed well. Brothers Benedict and Caleb were sinful proud."

"Whoop-de-do for them." Tobias takes a few steps toward the edge and looks down at the river. "Anybody ever jump?"

I tell him the story of Sister Salah.

I had the story from my mother, who knew it from Sister Agatha.

Salah was Father Grace's first wife, a woman of great beauty and intelligence, but with a crack in her soul. It was she who helped Father Grace to establish his first ministry, it was she who toiled by his side when Zerachiel led him to the Tree growing alone and neglected in the heart of Montana, and it was she who bore him his first son.

In those distant days, the Grace were few: Father Grace, Brothers Seth, Andrew, and Caleb, Sisters Salah and Agatha, and the children Mary, Yvonne, and Peter. It was they who harvested the trees to build the Hall of Enoch, who mortared the stones of the wall surrounding the Tree, and who excavated the underground shelters beneath what is now Elderlodge and Gracehome. It was they who dug the first well, and built the roads, and planted the first crops, and slaughtered the first lamb.

On the night of the full moon, in the month Abib, in the Hebrew Year 5741, a child was born to Salah. The child was called Adam, and Adam was well loved by all, and the Grace rejoiced.

The child grew quickly, walking at nine months, speaking at one year, and reading at four. By his seventh summer Adam had memorized Genesis. At the age of twelve he began preaching at the Grace Ministries, drawing great crowds of the curious and the devout. It was during that time that the number of Grace grew rapidly and Nodd began to flourish.

The next year, many of the Grace were struck with influenza. Young Adam spent hours at the bedsides of the stricken. Those to whom he ministered recovered quickly. Adam was not so fortunate. He took to his bed with a ferocious fever and never arose. The grief over his death was a terrible thing. A leaden pall settled over the land, and there was much weeping in Nodd. The once joyful Sister Salah suffered worst of all. According to Agatha, her joy turned to despair and her will to live crumpled.

The day after Adam's body was returned to the earth, Sister Salah walked alone up the Spine and never returned. Her shattered body, scavenged by vultures, was found several days later at the bottom of the gorge.

All that happened the year before my parents brought me to Nodd. Still, I sometimes imagine I can hear Salah's final, fading scream beneath the muffled roar of the rapids.

"I'd jump." Tobias sucks smoke from his cigarette, then lets the smoke stream out through his nostrils. "I mean, if I wanted to off myself."

"Why would you want to do that?"

He looks at me. "Lots of reasons. You don't ever think about it?"

"No!"

He laughs. "Me neither." He turns back toward the gorge and flicks his cigarette out over the edge. "Hardly ever."

8

At supper that night, Jerome approaches and tells me that
Brother Enos wishes to see me. My first thought is that Enos
has learned of my encounter with the Worldly girl.

"Now?" I say.

"After you have eaten," says Jerome. He returns to his
table.

"Who is Brother Enos?" Tobias asks.

"Archcherub Enos deals with Worldly matters," I say.
Enos has been of the Grace longer than anyone other than
Father Grace himself. "He is our director of security as well."

"You mean he's like the cult cop?"

I glare at him. He smiles and shrugs. I return to my meal
and finish quickly. I am not anxious to visit Enos, but I can see

no reason to delay the inevitable. Enos is most rigorous; I fear that my punishment will be harsh.

Enos is sitting behind his desk, packing a corncob pipe with tobacco from a leather pouch. I watch him carefully tamp down the tobacco leaves, place the pipe stem between his teeth, ignite a wooden match with a flick of his thumbnail, and draw the flame into the pipe bowl. The harsh tang of sulfur from the match is followed by the earthy aroma of burning leaves. Enos puffs until he is satisfied with the way his pipe is burning, then shakes the flame from the match. His dark-brown eyes fix upon me. "Sit, Brother Jacob," he says. His tone is crisp and flat. Although I know Enos to be the same age as my father, he looks older. His narrow face is all edges and hollows. Where Father Grace is a great sword of righteousness, Enos is the cutting edge.

I lift one of the chairs from its hook on the wall and place it before his desk.

"I understand you took the new boy out to the gorge," he says.

"It is true," I say.

"Why?"

"I wished to impress him," I say.

Enos draws on his pipe, his eyes locked on mine. I can almost hear the sweat coming from my pores.

"Was he impressed?"

"He did not much enjoy the walk."

Enos nods. "He is a troubled lad."

"I do not think he will be happy here."

"Be that as it may be, he is here." Enos sighs and sinks back in his chair, and for a moment I see the weariness concealed beneath his hard exterior. "The boy's sister may be a problem as well."

I feel myself starting to relax. Brother Enos is confiding in me. That is a good sign.

"The Lord will show us the way," I say.

"Perhaps. Still, we may have brought a nest of serpents into our midst." He frowns into his pipe, fires another match, and relights it. "He will take watching."

"He says he will not be staying long. He says he is going to live with his father."

"That is unlikely. His father abandoned his family eight years ago."

"He says his father lives in Costa Rica."

"Interesting, if true. Is there anything else you wish to tell me?"

Again, for a moment, I am certain he knows of my conversation with Lynna, then I realize he is still asking about Tobias.

"He is angry," I say. "He clings to his old life. He does not wish to give up his Worldly garb."

Enos nods and taps the ashes out of his pipe. "I will ask Brother Peter to use him in the mill. Hard work will set the boy to rights." He reaches into his desk and comes out holding a small folded paper packet between two long fingers. "Tonight you will bring him sweet tea. Put the contents of this into his cup and see that he drinks it. It will help him sleep." I want to ask why, but Enos's tone tells me it is not the time for questions. I take the tiny packet and fold it into my sleeve.

Brother Enos looks at his pocket watch. He is one of the few Grace to carry such a device. "It is almost time for Evensong," he says. "G'bless."

Evensong is well attended that night; the Grace are all curious to see the new arrivals at close hand. Our voices are many and strong. Tobias and I sit near the back of the hall, across the aisle from his mother and sister. He does not participate, but only sits silently with his prayer book unopened on his lap. Several times I see one or another of the unmarried Sisters turning their heads to look at him. I watch, hoping to catch a glimpse of Ruth. I cannot find her at first, then I spot her near the front of the hall when she pretends to drop her book, reaches down, and as she bends looks back past her shoulder. Her eyes find us, Tobias and me. She looks quickly away.

Afterward, in Menshome, I bring Tobias his sullied tea.

That night I dream. I am following Ruth up the Spine. I am calling to her but she will not look back, and her scarf blows off and I try to catch it but the wind twists it from my grasp, and she laughs, and it is Lynna's laugh, and I see that we are standing at the Knob and it is not Ruth at all, but Lynna, and her hair is loose and her robe is open and her feet are bare, and the roar of the Pison fills my ears.

When I awaken I find I have spilled my seed onto my nightclothes. I rise and head for the lavatory. With dawn still hours away, I cleanse myself in the cold trickle of water from the basin, then return to bed and close my eyes and silently recite the Prayer of Expiation.

Forgive me, O Lord, though I am the least of
your creatures.
Forgive me though I have transgressed.
Forgive me . . .

My thoughts drift. As the words scroll across my consciousness, I imagine crisp, pine-scented air filling my lungs, the sound of wind in the trees, my feet trodding the familiar, well-worn path, the sun warm on my back, the chain-link fence brushing my shoulder . . . and my thoughts once again become dreams.

I awaken at first light. Tobias is stirring in the next cell. He coughs. I hear him hack and spit. Then I hear him cursing, using words I have never before heard. I walk barefoot from my cell. Tobias is standing naked in his doorway. His loins are nearly hairless. I look away, thinking he must be younger than I had thought.

"Where are my clothes?" he asks, half angry, half scared.

"In the drawer beneath your pallet," I tell him. Last night, after drinking his tea, Tobias had nearly fallen asleep at the common table. Will and I had walked him back to his cell and laid him upon his pallet, fully clothed. Enos must have sent some Higher Cherubim to disrobe him as he slept.

He goes back into his cell, and I hear more cursing. Several Brothers have awakened and are peering from their cells, their expressions ranging from shocked to amused. I return to my cell and finish dressing. When I come out again, Tobias has dressed himself in work garb, stiff and new. The trousers are several inches too long, as are his sleeves. He is agitated.

"You will need to roll up your cuffs and sleeves," I say.

"What I *need* is my *clothes* back!" He practically spits out the words. "And my other stuff, too."

"You will have to ask Brother Enos," I say.

"My iPod, my knife, my notebook — they even took my toothpaste!"

"All you need will be provided."

"Yeah? Well, I need my stuff right *now*. Where do I find this Enos guy?"

I imagine how Brother Enos might react, and I smile.

"You think this is funny?" He puts a palm on my chest and shoves; I stagger backward and almost fall. I want to push him back, but I control myself. Tobias looks at the other Brothers staring wide-eyed from their doorways. He zeros in on Will. "What are *you* looking at?"

Will laughs. I know he is laughing out of nervousness, but Tobias takes it the wrong way. He punches Will hard in the face.

Fistfights are rare amongst the Grace; I have known them to occur only between the younger boys. When I was but seven I fought with Luke over a toy he would not share. We were made to stand before the entire congregation and beg for forgiveness. It was profoundly humiliating.

A gush of blood spills from Will's nose. Tobias seems shocked by what he has done, but only for a moment, and then Will is swinging his thin arms, pummeling Tobias about the neck and shoulders. He is taller than Tobias, but Tobias outweighs him. Tobias strikes back, hammering a fist into Will's cheek. Will lurches back; Tobias kicks him in the knee. Will lets out a howl and collapses. Tobias kicks him again, this time in the face. I throw myself between them and wrap my arms around Tobias; he falls backward and I land on top of him. Men are shouting and Tobias is struggling mightily. A pair of strong hands grabs my shoulders and pulls me off him.

The fight lasted only seconds, but the noise was enough to bring Brothers Jerome and Benedict at a run. It is Jerome who holds me now, his grip painfully tight. Benedict is bending over Will, assessing his injuries. Tobias climbs to his feet, uttering more curses. Benedict gives him a shocked look.

"Brother, seal thy lips!" he says.

Tobias tells him to go to Hell, a terrible curse that causes Brother Benedict to blanch.

Jerome releases me and attempts to take Tobias by the arm, but Tobias shakes him off. "I want my clothes and my stuff back. Now!"

"Peace on you, Brother." Jerome speaks softly, as if coaxing a skittish calf.

"Piss on yourself! I'm not anybody's brother!" Tobias squares his shoulders and clenches his fists as if expecting Jerome to attack him, but Jerome simply sets his features in a flat smile.

Brother Benedict helps Will to his feet. His nose is already swelling; there is a cut on his cheek. "We had best see Brother Samuel," Benedict says. "Can you walk?"

Will nods, but when he tries to put weight on his left leg he nearly collapses. Beads of pain sweat appear on his forehead.

"Lean on me," Benedict says, and they hobble off together on three legs. Tobias looks scornfully after them.

"Your Worldly goods are safe with Brother Enos," Jerome says.

"Where do I find this Enos guy?" Tobias is sounding less frightened and more confident. He believes he has power, that he is different from the rest of us. I am sorry for him, but also discover within myself a trickle of unclean joy at the price he will pay.

"I will take you to him," Jerome says.

9

All through the day, as Luke and I repair fences in the south meadow, I am beset by feelings of anger and guilt over the events of that morning. I did not need to show amusement at Tobias's discomfiture. I could have calmed him, perhaps. Still, it was he who struck the first blows. I think of Will, his nose stuffed with cotton, lying in his cell with ice packs on his swollen knee, and I blame him, too, for laughing at Tobias, and for failing to defend himself. We are all sinners.

It is late afternoon when Lynna slips into my mind, and I realize that I have not thought of her in many hours.

"Brother!" Luke calls to me. He is struggling to reset a damaged post. I go to him and hold the post steady. As he pounds the soil firm around its base, I send up a silent prayer of thanks. The Lord has sent Tobias here for a reason. Before his arrival, I had been beset by thoughts of the Worldly girl, but now I am thinking of Tobias, and Lynna seems unreal and distant.

"I wonder how he is," I say.

"Who? Brother Will?" Luke gives the post a shake.

"My thoughts were of the new boy."

Luke gives me a curious look. "It was Will who was injured. Samuel says he may never fully recover from the damage to his knee."

"Tobias does not know our ways," I say. "He was frightened and confused."

"A few days in the Pit will do him good."

"Perhaps." I think of Tobias in the Praying Pit beneath the Tower, a bare cubicle used voluntarily by some penitents, and more rarely for the punishment of the unrepentant or dangerously disturbed. The last time the Pit was used for involuntary detention was four summers ago, when Brother Von, Father Grace's son, sneaked into Womenshome and hid in the rafters above their bathing pool. Von was not right even then. He could learn neither numbers nor writing and could handle only the simplest of tasks, but he was happy, always full of laughter and joy, a boy in a man's body. His attempt to spy on the women was but the curiosity of a child.

Von was seen by Sister Louise. The women chased him out of the building, where he was subdued by several Higher Cherubim. Father Grace directed that Von, who had seventeen summers at the time, be confined to the Praying Pit. For several days, Von's cries and moans could be heard from beneath the Tower. It was a dark and disturbing time in Nodd. Finally Father Grace took Von to the infirmary, where Brother Samuel, our healer, performed an exorcism, and Von's anguished cries ceased. A few weeks later, Von was returned to Menshome with two livid scars beneath his brow. Some of the young men whisper that he is also missing something between his legs. I do not know if that is true, but he has troubled no one since that day. Nor has he laughed.

"We had best get moving lest we miss supper," Luke says.

I nod and sling the tool bag over my shoulder. As we continue our journey along the meadow fence, I wonder whether an exorcism might be performed on Tobias. The thought disturbs me as I think of the scars beneath Von's brow and the emptiness in his eyes.

I will pray for them both at Evensong.

The Cherubim are talking in low voices as Luke and I enter the dining area. Luke goes to sit with Jerome and Gregory. I set my tray near Will and Aaron. Aaron is talking about Tobias.

"He should be banished." Aaron is but a Lower Cherub, yet he makes this pronouncement as if he were already an Elder.

"I hope he is," Will says, his voice distorted by his swollen and bandaged nose.

"What about the sister and mother?" I ask.

"Father Grace would not wish to lose them as well," Aaron says.

"I would not miss them," Will says.

Aaron shrugs.

I eat my stew quickly and mechanically, hardly tasting it. When I have finished I go to Tobias's cell. As he said, all his possessions have been confiscated. On a hunch, I reach my hand into the space behind his mattress and run my hand along it until I feel something hard. I lift out a small red-and-white cardboard box bearing the inscription *Marlboro*. Inside are six cigarettes and a green plastic lighter. The pounding of my heart feels hollow, as if my viscera has been replaced by nothingness. I close my eyes and focus on breathing until my heartbeat slows, then tuck the cigarette packet into my sleeve, take it to my cell, and hide it at the back of my drawer. It is most strange, to watch myself perform these acts. I wonder whether I am possessed, and if so, what demon or angel has attached itself to my soul.

Evensong is lightly attended that evening. Father Grace is not present, nor are any of the other Elders save for my father, who leads us in prayer. On the women's side I see Sister Ruth sitting with her mother, Sister Naomi. The eldest Sisters are present, as always: Agatha, Yvonne, Marianne, and the widow Dalva, all sitting at the front. My mother is there as well. On the men's side are Peter, the youngest of the Archcherubim, who manages our livestock and crops; Caleb, who teaches us numbers; the Higher Cherubim Jerome, John, and Taylor, and a half dozen Lower Cherubim, including myself. Von is sitting off by himself, munching on something he has hidden in his sleeve. Will has chosen not to come, for which I cannot blame him, as he must still be feeling poorly.

I follow the prayers automatically. I tell myself I am there to pray for the souls of Tobias and Brother Von, yet even as my mouth forms the proper words, my thoughts drift. I think of cities and oceans; I think of airplanes and cars and trains; I think of the moon. I think of Tobias casting his cigarette butt into the gorge; I think of Sister Salah. I think of Worldly girls with sun in their hair. Was it only days ago I spoke with Lynna?

I open my eyes to find myself back in the Hall of Enoch. My eyes drift to the right and touch upon Sister Ruth. As if sensing my thoughts of her, she turns her head and looks at me. Her teeth flash white. I feel the blood rush to my face, and elsewhere.

After Evensong I return to Menshome. Most of the men gather in the common room to share stories and gossip. I retire to my cell and lie on my back, arms rigid at my sides. I close my eyes and see Ruth's smile. My hand rises, reaching for her, and for a moment my fingers feel the soft skin of her cheek, and her hair slips from beneath her scarf. It is not the wisp of chestnut brown I have glimpsed before but a thick shock of sun-bleached blond.

"No." My own voice startles me. I open my eyes. I am alone.

I think of Brother Von hiding in the rafters of Womenshome, looking down upon the bathing pool, waiting for the Sisters to reveal their secrets, and I imagine that I am him. Was it such a terrible thing he did? Perhaps it was, for while I sometimes follow my mind deep into those places, I do not go there in the flesh. Is that all that separates me from Von? That paper-thin moment when sinful thought crosses over into sins of the flesh? What then of Lynna, the Worldly girl? Though we never touched, though we are separated by miles of chain-link fence, I feel her presence.

I force myself to mouth a silent prayer of cleansing and abstinence. The Lord must hear me with one ear because when I close my eyes again, Lynna is gone. Instead, the image that hovers before me is that of Tobias.

I lie awake until all the others have retired, and the lights are out, and the symphony of their snores echoes from the rafters. When I judge all of Menshome to be dreaming, I rise silently and take the package of cigarettes from my drawer and let myself out, even as I pray for forgiveness for the sin that I am about to commit.

10

The Village on this moonless night is still and silent as a cat in ambush. A low light flickers from one window in Elderlodge. Elsewhere the compound is all deep grays and pitch-black. I make my way past Elderlodge to the Tower, where I kneel outside the low, barred window at its base. I hear the scurry of some small creature in the grass: a vole, or perhaps a wood rat.

No sound issues from within the Pit.

Brother Benedict has taught us that there is a point in every mortal transgression when the mind, the heart, and the soul clash. I never understood that before, but now I feel the battle raging within as I kneel before the low window and peer into the darkness.

"Tobias!" I whisper.

Nothing. Then a rustling sound, and I see the shadow of his face looking out at me. "Who's that?" he asks.

"Brother Jacob."

I hear him breathe in and out.

"Get lost," he says. But he keeps his voice low, and his fingers curl around the bars.

"I brought you something."

More breathing. "What?"

I remove the cigarette package from my sleeve and hold it out to him. He takes it.

"You smoke any?" he asks.

"No," I say. I hear him fumbling with the cigarettes, then a flare of light illuminates his face as he thumbs the lighter. I smell smoke. Each time he inhales, the tip of the cigarette becomes bright enough that I can see his face.

"How come?" he asks.

"How come what?"

"How come you're being nice to me?"

I shrug, then realize he probably can't see me. "I thought you might need them."

"I don't need them. I can quit anytime."

"I am sorry that you are here in this place."

"They can't keep me here forever."

I think of Von. "You must repent."

"Repent for what? They took my stuff!"

"Did Brother Enos speak with you?"

"The dude with the face like a hatchet?"

"Yes." I almost smile at his description.

"Him and the other guy, the fat one."

"Brother Samuel."

"Yeah. They've both been talking to me. Reading the Bible and stuff. I think they're trying to brainwash me. I told them I wanted my stuff back."

"Do not provoke Brother Samuel," I say, thinking of the surgery he visited upon Brother Von. "Tell them you are sorry and that you wish to make amends."

"Why? I didn't *do* anything!"

"You attacked Brother Will."

"He was laughing at me."

"He meant nothing by it. He is badly injured. Brother Samuel says he has torn the tendons in his knee."

Tobias puffs furiously on his cigarette. The glowing tip is quite long. After a time, he speaks.

"So I just say I'm sorry? And they'll let me out?"

"That is my hope."

"And what if I run to the cops and tell them you guys locked me up?"

"The police are of the World. Nodd is of the Lord."

Tobias snorts dismissively. "In Colorado Springs, they never said nothing about locking people up or everybody dressing the same. They were all, like, love and peace and nature." He draws again on his cigarette. "I should've known this place was bogus. I mean, the church was in a mini-mall, between a Chinese restaurant and a dry cleaner. Used to be a donut shop, but they closed 'cause of the dry-cleaning smell."

"What church?"

"Grace Ministries. It was the most rinky-dink operation you can imagine. I couldn't believe my mom was taking it serious."

I am surprised by this. I imagined our ministries as being large, beautiful buildings, like the Hall of Enoch.

"One-Eye—Father Grace—he wasn't all scary, like he is here. He had on regular clothes, and a patch over his eye, and his hair was tied back, and he kept talking about Nodd as a sanctuary, like he was a salesman for some exclusive resort. He was like, 'Come to Nodd, live off the land in peace and security, and all your problems will go away.'

"My mom was totally into it. I figured it was just one of her phases, you know? She used to be all into this Jesus Saves church, and before that it was Scientology. I guess Kari getting knocked up pushed Mom over the edge. Me getting thrown in jail didn't help, either."

"You were imprisoned?"

"Just for a couple days. It was no big deal. I borrowed a car from some guy and he called the cops. Anyway, when my mom started talking seriously about coming here, I looked up the Grace online. There are congressmen and stuff investigating. They say you're a cult."

"We are not a cult."

"Whatever. I just want to get out of here."

I do not know if he means he wants out of the Pit, or out of Nodd. I fear to ask.

"I am sorry you are troubled," I say. I hear a sound and look behind me. I see the dark shape of someone walking from Menshome to the lavatory. Probably Brother Benedict, whose bladder is weak. I lower my voice further and whisper, "Even if you do not truly regret your sins, you must repent, or it will go poorly for you."

"Okay! All right already!"

"Hush. Brother Benedict is up and about."

We wait in silence for Brother Benedict to leave the lavatory and return to Menshome. I am trying to understand how I have come to risk being caught talking to Tobias, bringing him cigarettes, and suggesting that he bear false witness to Brother Enos. This Worldly boy, filled with anger and sin, has done me no great service, yet I feel responsible. Perhaps it is that when think of him, I am able to push aside the dull ache that threatens to consume me when I think of Ruth, and the other, sharper pangs brought on by thinking of Lynna.

"You still there?" Tobias whispers.

"I am." I hear anger in my voice.

"What's the matter?"

"Nothing." It is not his fault that I have sinned. "Benedict is returning to Menshome. I will wait a few minutes for him to settle, then I must go."

The lighter sparks, and he sets fire to another cigarette.

The next several days are busy. I am put to work harvesting sorghum, separating the seed heads, fodder for our milk cows, from the stalks, which we press for syrup and molasses. Sorghum is our main source of sweetener. I am accustomed to the earthy flavor, although I much prefer wild honey. Last year Brother Taylor discovered a large beehive in a lightning-blasted cottonwood, and for months afterward we had honey. I always watch now for bees and note the direction they take. I believe there is a hive somewhere on the Spine, but I have yet to find it.

I think of Tobias often. The day after he was placed in the Pit, the Brothers talked of little else. But as the days pass, as Brother Will's wounds heal, the drama of that violent morning fades from memory. By the time a week has passed, the Brothers act as if Tobias does not exist. Still, I cannot forget that he is there, and I keep thinking about the scars above Brother Von's dead eyes.

On Manday night I cannot sleep. I once again creep out of Menshome and visit the Praying Pit.

11

As I near the Tower, I hear a man's voice. I stop, holding my breath. The voice is coming from inside the Pit. I listen carefully. It sounds like Father Grace, but thinner, without the power he brings to his words. I walk softly to the base of the Tower, get down on my hands and knees, and crawl to the window.

It is definitely Father Grace's voice, but I sense that it is not Father Grace himself. It is a recording of one of his sermons. I hear another sound as well. Snoring. I press my face against the bars and attempt to look inside, but the darkness is utter and impenetrable.

"Tobias!" I whisper. The snoring continues. I find a small stone and toss it toward the sound. I hear a sudden snort, then sounds of movement. "Tobias!" I say again.

A few seconds later, pale fingers grasp the bars and I can see the smear of his face.

"Jacob?"

I am vastly relieved to hear his voice.

"Yes, it is me. Are you well?"

"I'm okay. . . . No, actually I'm going nuts in here. They make me listen to this stuff all night. I have to stuff cheese in my ears to sleep."

"Cheese?"

"It's all I got. And they make me read the Bible all day. How long are they gonna keep me here?"

"Did you repent?"

"I said I was sorry. I don't think Enos believes me. Also, he smelled the cigarettes and found the butts."

"You must repent!"

"I tried — I *told* you."

"You must try harder."

"Okay . . . Have you seen my mom?"

"She is well. I saw both her and your sister at Evensong."

"Can you ask her to talk to Enos? Or Father Grace?"

I think for a moment. For me to approach Tobias's mother would be unseemly. In any case, I doubt that her words would sway Brother Enos.

"You must repent in your heart," I say. "It is the only way."

"Screw you, then! Did they send you here just to tell me that?"

"No one sent me. I should not be here at all." I back away from the window and stand up.

"Jacob, wait!"

I walk away.

The next night, I return to the Pit and hear from within a recording of a call-and-response from Babel Hour:

"And he shall kill the bullock before the Lord . . ."

"And the priests shall bring the blood . . ."

I lie on my belly with my face near the bars. "Tobias!" I whisper.

"And he shall flay the burnt offering . . ."

"And cut it into pieces . . ."

Tobias's hands grasp the bars.

"Hey," he says. "I'm sorry I yelled at you."

"Did you repent?"

"I tried. Like I told you, Enos doesn't believe me. I think he wants me to memorize the Bible first or something. . . . What is this I'm listening to?"

"It is from Leviticus. A call-and-response from Babel Hour."

"What's that?"

I explain to him about Babel Hour.

"That's how you meet girls here?" he says.

"And the sons of Aaron the priest shall put fire upon the altar . . ."

"Yes. It is great fun."

"Weird," he says, not in a nasty, disdainful way, but with a sense of amazement.

"How did you meet girls in Limon?" I ask.

"Everywhere. In school, or at the mall. Lots of ways. I met Shelly in Sunday school."

"Shelly?"

"My girlfriend. Ex-girlfriend, I guess. She was cool."

"Tell me of her."

He tells me about the girl Shelly, about her long yellow hair, her eyes the color of the sky, her breasts —

"You saw them with your eyes?" I say in wonder.

"Sure. We used to make out all the time."

"Make out?"

"You know, feel her up and stuff."

"You touched her body?" The thought of it is shocking and unbearably thrilling. I have hardly dared to imagine such a thing.

"Every inch," he says. I hear pride, not shame, in his voice.

We talk for a long time. As the machine plays verses from Exodus, he tells me of girls, of the Internet, of movies and video games and cars and strange foods. He tells me about his father, living in the jungles of Costa Rica, and of his sister's pregnancy. "She wanted to marry her boyfriend, but he was only seventeen, and then she was going to give up the baby for adoption, but Mom started going to Grace Ministries, and we ended up here."

I tell him about walking the fence, and hunting deer in the High Forest, and winter storms, and swimming in the ice-cold waters of the Pison.

I tell him about how I met Lynna.

"She sounds cool," he says, and I wish I had not spoken of her.

I tell him of the Tree.

"You mean like in the Garden of Eden?"

"Yes. Father Grace sometimes calls our land Eden West. The first Garden of Eden was the beginning. Nodd's gardens will bloom at the End of Days."

"Huh." I hear doubt in his voice.

"The Tree grows in the Sacred Heart. It is the reason we are here. When you get out, I will show it to you."

"If they ever *let* me out."

"Do as Enos asks, and you will be freed."

"And that which remaineth of the flesh . . ."

"And of the bread shall ye burn —"

The recording ends with a loud click. We are startled into silence. After a few seconds, Tobias says, "In the morning Enos starts it up again."

"I should go," I say.

"See you tomorrow?"

"I will try," I say.

The next day, after I deliver my last bundle of sorghum stalks to the press, Brother Enos sends for me. As I enter his office his expression is stern, even for Enos. I fear that Tobias has told him of my visits.

He does not ask me to sit. That is a bad sign. In his hand he holds a scrap of yellow paper. He looks from me to the paper, and back again.

"Brother Jacob, is there anything you wish to confess?" he asks.

His words cut me like a knife; I feel as if my insides are about to spill out onto the floor. It is all I can do to remain standing. A faint, tight smile compresses Enos's lips. "I see," he says.

"I am afraid for him," I say. "I told him to repent."

Enos's brow furrows at that, and I realize that he expected me to say something else.

"Explain yourself," he says sharply.

"I . . . I went to visit the new boy last night. In the Pit."

"Why would you do that?"

"I fear for his soul," I say. It is true, or at least half true. "I feel . . . I feel I am responsible for him being there."

"How so?"

"I was tasked with showing him our ways. I failed. And now he pays the price."

"Price? He pays no *price*. He is being rewarded with salvation."

"As was Brother Von?"

Enos's face darkens. I cannot believe that I said what I said.

"Brother Von was possessed. His trespass at Womenshome was but the final straw. The Grace suffered years of Von's transgressions before that night. We had no alternative but to have Samuel perform an exorcism. The boy Tobias is merely ignorant and undisciplined—as are you."

He waits for me to respond, but I am too terrified to

84

speak, not knowing what might come out of my treacherous mouth. Brother Enos makes an exasperated sound with his lips, then looks again at the scrap of yellow paper.

"This was discovered by Brother Luke. It was attached to the north fence." Brother Enos impales me with his raptor eyes and holds out the paper. "Do you know anything about it?"

My stomach goes hollow as I read the scrawled and damning message:

Hey, Cult Boy!
How's it going?
Whassup?
—Lynna

12

I lie.

I do not know how I do it, but I lie to Brother Enos. I tell him that I know nothing of the note, neither who wrote it nor for whom it was written. He believes me, possibly because I just admitted to visiting Tobias.

"Has Brother Will said anything about meeting a girl?" he asks.

"He has said nothing to me."

He frowns at the note in his hand. "There is a child named Evelyn who lives on the Rocking K. I imagine this 'Lynna' to be her. Have you met anyone on your patrols? Anyone at all?"

"I would have reported it to you."

"Of course you would. As you reported your visit to the boy Tobias."

I say nothing.

"You will not visit him again."

I nod.

"I will bring your transgression to Father Grace. He will assign you penance. G'bless."

I leave his office on jellied knees, expecting him to call me back at any moment, expecting him to beat me and throw me in the Pit with Tobias, expecting Zerachiel to appear before me wielding his sword of flame, to send me spinning headless into the Void.

My fears are not realized; I am left only with my shame.

I do not have long to wait to receive my penance. Brother Jerome delivers an envelope to me at supper. Inside is a short note. There is to be no beating, no public confession, no shaming, no examination of my soul. I suspect that Father Grace does not wish Tobias's incarceration to be on the minds of all the Grace.

Instead, I am to kneel before the Tree at last light and pray aloud until the sun once again strikes its topmost branches.

You will speak of this to no one but the Lord, the note ends, followed by Enos's spiky signature.

I pray for Tobias; I pray for my own sullied soul.

Does the Lord hear me, or am I truly alone here? My knees are on fire, the cold seeps into my body through every pore, the leaves of the Tree shift and rustle in the wind. Through the branches I see the new moon, rising up over the high hedge that protects the Sacred Heart.

My voice, raspy and weak, is swallowed by the night.

I pray for redemption, I pray for forgiveness, I pray for the Ark to come. I pray for rain, that I might tip my head back and let the drops flow down my parched throat. I pray for all the sinners of the World, I pray for Von, I pray for dawn. It must be well past midnight when I hear soft footsteps behind me. I continue to pray as the footsteps draw closer, then stop.

"Brother Jacob." The voice is high, soft, and familiar; I feel my heart clench.

"Father?" I have spoken privately to Father Grace only once before, on the day I was made a Cherub.

He seats himself on the wall. I keep my eyes upon the Tree, grateful that I do not have to look into his eye.

"Your prayers are strong," he says. "I have been listening."

"Thank you, Father."

"Your concern for the new boy does you credit."

"It was wrong of me to go to him."

"Many sins are born of good intentions."

"Yes, Father."

"Enos and Peter praise your industry and dedication."

I bow my head. "That is good to hear."

"The boy will remain, for a time, in the Praying Pit."

"Yes, Father."

"Yet I sense you question the need of it."

"I am sorry," I say miserably, knowing he can read my heart.

"The fact is, young Jacob, there is a storm brewing in Helena, where the politicians weave their wicked webs. The World beats at our gate. Those who would see the Grace sundered and scattered are amassing. We must stand together if we are to survive. We must speak with one voice. Our Faith is our future. We must be as one."

I do not understand what Father Grace is telling me. He senses this, and continues.

"They will descend upon us—the politicians, the police, the media. They come in hopes of destroying us. We must present a unified front."

"Why should we allow them in at all?" I ask.

"If we do not open our gates to them, they threaten to take us by force."

"Why?"

"They twist their Worldly laws to advance their dark agenda. They say we harbor weapons, that we abuse our children, that we are evil upon this land."

"That is not true!" I say.

"Truth is nothing to such people. Still, if we stand together, they have no power. The boy Tobias is an unknown quantity; I fear he will tell lies about us. He must remain in confinement until he understands the error of his ways."

"He repented to Brother Enos," I hear myself say in a small voice.

Father Grace does not reply immediately, then his hand cups my shoulder and squeezes gently. It is warm; I feel his heat radiating from my shoulder into my core.

"You have a good heart, Jacob. Would that all men felt such love of their fellows. Do not worry about the boy. He will not be harmed."

"How long must he stay there?" I ask.

"Only until his heart becomes whole." As he speaks the words, I know them to be true, and my own heart swells with gratitude.

"Yes, Father."

He lifts his hand from my shoulder, and I feel the loss of it.

"When the Ark comes, you will be welcomed by Zerachiel with open arms. Repeat the Arbor Prayer three times, then return to your cell and sleep well. May the Lord be with you always." Father Grace stands. "G'bless."

I hear his footsteps receding.

I speak the Arbor Prayer.

The next day, Father Grace calls a Convocation. As we gather, there is much whispering. No one seems to know why we are meeting. I suspect that Father Grace is going to tell us of the impending visit from the Worldly folk, but I am wrong.

The Convocation begins with Elder Abraham leading us in the Prayer of Joining. This is a hopeful sign, for it is the prayer used for espousals, baptisms, and the elevation of Cherubim. Father Grace, his wives, and his girl children are seated beside the pulpit. Von is seated with the congregation, picking at his nose while staring blankly into space. I search the Sisters' side of the hall for Sister Ruth, but I cannot see her. After the prayer, Father Grace rises.

"Brethren, I have joyful news. The Lord has spoken to me, and He has told me that I am to take a new wife, and she is to bear me a son."

A murmur ripples through the congregation. This is good news indeed, for although Father Grace loves and treasures his girl children, we all know that he desires a boy child above all else. I look at Von's vacant face. Does he comprehend any of this? Father Grace's three wives sit beside him with their faces carefully composed. I turn my attention to the unmarried women, wondering who it will be. Could it be Sister Judith, Tobias's mother? Is she young enough to bear another child? Perhaps it will be Olivia or Louise, who have waited longest to be betrothed.

Father Grace spreads his arms wide and speaks a prayer of thanks, then extends one hand toward the congregation. One of the Sisters stands and climbs the three steps to kneel before Father Grace. She rises and embraces him, then turns to face us.

It is Sister Ruth.

My ears are filled with a soundless roar as Father Grace's wives gather to embrace their newest member. I tear my eyes away and see my mother looking at me from across the aisle, her face soft with pity. I squeeze my eyes closed. I tell myself to breathe. I feel a touch on my shoulder. It is Will, who knows of my feelings for Ruth. I shrug off his hand. I want to run from the hall, to take myself across the field to the Spine, to follow Sister Salah into the gorge.

Somehow, I do not. I remain, I sit, and I pray. I push the pain and fury and shame into a hard knot and hold it suspended, a bag of broken granite dangling in place of my heart.

As the Convocation draws to a close, I sense Will's worried looks, but I keep my face still as frozen water. Father Grace descends and walks down the aisle, followed by his wives: Marianne, Juliette, Fara . . . and now Ruth. I fix my eyes upon her as she passes. She does not look at me, but the prideful, smug, self-satisfied curve of her lips tells me more than I wish to know.

Back at Menshome I retire to my cell and am left alone, as alone as Tobias in the Pit. I lie curled on my pallet, waiting in vain for sleep to take me. I keep seeing Ruth's face as she paraded down the aisle with the wives. I meant nothing to her. I am embarrassed, I am ashamed, I am furious, but most of all I feel powerless. There is nothing I can do to undo that which is done. They are wed. They were wed the moment Father Grace declared it to be so; such is our custom.

As my thoughts swirl and begin to cohere, I realize that my desire for Ruth, so strongly felt for so many years, has left me. She is not who I thought her to be. The thought of touching her now repels me, and so I turn my anger upon myself, for it was I who allowed myself to care for her.

Sleep does not come. It is well past midnight when I rise and walk outside. I move through the darkness to the Tower and press my face to the barred window of the Pit. It is silent inside: no recording, no snoring, no sound at all. I call out for Tobias. Nothing. I gather a handful of pebbles, reach through the bars, and toss them toward the pallet where he sleeps. No response. I call out again. I throw more pebbles.

Nothing.

Tobias is gone.

3

Their spirit is full of lust, that they
may be punished in their body.
—Enoch 67:8

13

I am awakened by Brother Jerome standing in the doorway to my cell, poking me with the handle of a broom.

"Brother," he says.

I open one eye. It is still dark outside. I swat away the broom handle.

"Brother, it is fourth Landay."

Fourth Landay? I sit up, rubbing my eyes.

"It cannot be," I say.

"It is. You patrol today."

I groan. I must have slept, but it could not have been for long. Thoughts of Tobias and Ruth and Father Grace kept me up most of the night, and now I am faced with a day-long walk.

"Brother Gregory has reported a breach in the north-central section," Jerome says. Gregory has taken Will's edge-walking duties while Will waits for his knee to heal.

"Why then did Gregory not repair it himself?" I ask.

"He was not equipped. You will need a shovel. Do not delay. There is weather coming."

Ordinarily I welcome the walk, but the events of last night weigh upon me so heavily that I fear I will be unable to bear them as I make my solitary trek. I consider going to Enos and telling him I am ill. Would he believe me? I do not think so. With leaden movements, I dress and prepare my backpack: wire, wire cutters, a folding shovel, and other fence-maintenance items. I take a thick slice of soda bread, a wedge of hard cheese, and a honeyed seedcake. I fill my water bottle. I fetch a carbine from the arms locker.

By the time I hoist my pack onto my shoulders, the Cherubim are stirring, and I am suddenly glad to be leaving. I do not need their morning banter and their pitying looks, and the eastern sky is brightening with the promise of day.

The borders of Nodd may be walked in many ways. The usual route is to take the road to the North Gate, then follow the fence east or west, depending on wind and whim. Sometimes I follow the trail through the High Meadow past Shepherd's Rock to the fence, a slightly longer but more pleasant route. Today I choose to head west, up the Spine to the Pison, then north along the edge of the gorge and down into the Mire. The land drops quickly. The rocky trail becomes green and moist, and soon I am at a level with the Pison where the river mingles with the Mire, becoming indefinite, sending fingers of water into a vast, boggy cedar swamp. When the water is high, as it often is in the spring, the bank of the river disappears completely, and one must pick one's way through the tangled morass, leaping from mossy rock to mossy tussock, walking along the trunks of fallen trees, finding shallow ridges of firmer ground, and occasionally sinking a foot deep into the bog. I have on more than one occasion found myself wet to the hip, struggling to free myself from the sucking peat.

This autumn the Lord has blessed us with weeks of dry weather, and the Mire is relatively dry. I move through a land of twisted cedars and willow, mosses and mushrooms, rotting logs and patches of marsh marigold, chittering squirrels and buzzing insects, always keeping the river in sight to my left, choosing each step with care. Some find the Mire to be a disturbing place, dark and deceitful. I have always enjoyed it. As I make my way across the spongy, treacherous surface, I feel a part of it, as if I am one of its creatures. As I walk, I keep seeing that smug smile on the face of Sister Ruth. It is clear to me that she is pleased with her sudden betrothal. Even more than pleased. How long has she known of Father Grace's intentions?

I think too about the storm that rose within me the moment I saw Ruth standing beside Father Grace. It must truly have been the hand of the Beast, as I imagined myself tearing handfuls of beard from Father Grace's face and pummeling him with my fists. Would I ever do such a thing? I would say I cannot imagine it, but I cannot, for I have done so.

A shadow passes over me; I look up to see a great gray owl drifting ghostlike through the trees, its broad wings slicing silently through the heavy air. The majestic beauty of it swells my throat. The owl alights high in a half-naked cedar a stone's throw away. I stand still as a statue, watching. I can see the bird's yellow eyes as it rotates its enormous head, searching for prey. Does it know I am here? Almost certainly it does, for wild creatures have an awareness that is beyond understanding.

I move toward it along a soft, mossy hump that was once a tree. The owl's eyes fix upon me. I am within a few steps of its tree when it spreads its wings and, effortlessly, lets the air carry it off to another perch. It is as if the bird wants me to follow.

Three times, the owl lets me get close before flying off to find a new branch, always within sight. Finally it tires of our game, and with a few powerful, soundless beats of its wings, it sails deep into the misty tangle of trees and is gone.

I look around and realize that I am not sure where I am. The sun has disappeared behind a haze of cloud, and I do not know in which direction the river lies. It is not big thing, I decide. The Mire is less than a mile on a side; if I walk in a straight line, I will eventually come out of it. I choose the same direction as the owl, and I walk.

An hour later, wet to my knees from stepping into a

sinkhole, I emerge from the Mire. The land rises swiftly, the cedars give way to juniper and pine, and I recognize the rocky wall of the northern escarpment. I pick my way up the steepening slope and am soon standing above the Mire on the southern verge of the High Meadow. A mist is drifting down from the low clouds, blurring the landscape. Far to the north, the shorter grasslands of the Rocking K rise up to meet the low sky. I can see the faint outline of the stone shelter known as Shepherd's Rock jutting from a knoll half a mile to my right.

The right and proper thing to do, I know, is to follow the escarpment back to the Pison, and from there walk the edge to the north fence. But I have already lost an hour or more wandering through the Mire, my feet are sodden, I have a fence to repair, and the mist is turning to drizzle. I head for the shelter.

The High Meadow feeds our sheep and cattle during the late spring and early summer, when the days are long and the sun is high. Late summer and fall, it lies fallow and is used only by mule deer and pronghorn. The grasses have grown tall these past two months; they tug at my thighs as I push through them. By the time I reach the stone shelter, the drizzle has become rain and I am soaked to the skin. I am pleased to see that the shelter has been stocked with dry wood. The steel drum inside contains matches, water, and kindling. I make a fire in the brazier, strip off my wet trousers, tunic, socks, and boots, and hang them near the fire. I drag the wooden bench close to the fire and sit naked and miserable to watch my clothing dry.

I am thinking about Ruth. I am thinking about my mother and the words she said to me not a week ago, during the corn harvest, when we spoke of Ruth: *I pray there are others you look favorably upon as well.* Had she known then that Father Grace intended to take Ruth for his own? And who else would she have me "look upon"? Rebecca, with her long nose and crossed eyes? Beryl, who is but fourteen? Louise, who at age eighteen cannot yet bake a decent muffin? My thoughts grow dark with resentment; my anger spills from Father Grace to Ruth herself, for taking such obvious pleasure in her new role. I feel resentment toward my mother as well, even though I know she wants only good things for me. And Tobias . . . wherever he is, I am angry with him as well, as his arrival in Nodd seems to have unleashed this plague of misery.

I sit until I can no longer stand to be alone with myself in that fieldstone shack with the tallowy smell of wet wool and wood smoke. I dress myself in my not-quite-dry garments. The rain has stopped, and the eastern sky shows patches of blue. Rather than follow the escarpment back to the Pison, I head directly north, skipping the northwest corner. I have never before skimped on my patrol. No one will ever know. It is a secret between myself and the Lord, which I find oddly satisfying.

By the time I reach the fence the sun has appeared in all its glory. I take it as a sign. If the Lord objected to my minor shortcut, would he not have responded with thunder and lightning? I know that I am thinking wrongly, but I do not care.

By noon the sky is nearly cloudless, and I come upon the breach reported by Brother Gregory. A marmot or some other creature has burrowed beneath the chain-link. Other creatures have used the access as well. I see coyote scat and a tuft of fur that may have come from a jackrabbit. I can repair it easily with a few rocks and some packed earth. That Gregory did not do so is testament to his innate laziness.

I shrug off my pack and go in search of some rocks. A short distance away, I find an outcropping of broken shale and manage to pry off a few chunks of the gray stone. I pick up the largest rock I can lift and am carrying it back toward the fence when I hear the whine of an engine. The sound is coming from the other side. A moment later I see a dark-green ATV bounce up over a low rise, following the cattle-worn trail paralleling the fence. The rider is wearing a flapping white canvas jacket and a bright-green helmet that does not quite contain her long blond hair. She sees me, skids to a stop, takes off her helmet, and shakes out her hair.

"Cult Boy," she says with a grin. "It must be Tuesday!"

14

"It is fourth *Landay,*" I say.

"Oh, yeah—*Lan*day." Lynna climbs down off the ATV and walks toward me. I step back. She stops two paces from the fence and gives me a puzzled smile. "I don't bite," she says.

"I did not think you were going to bite."

She looks at my pack on the ground, and at the shovel, and at the marmot hole beneath the fence.

"Trying to dig your way out?"

I shake my head, astonished that she would think I wanted to leave Nodd.

"Did you get my note?" she asks.

"Yes. Brother Luke found it and gave it to Brother Enos, who showed it to me. Please do not do that again."

"Why not?" She steps up to the fence and puts her fingers through the chain-link. I force myself not to back away. Her fingernails are painted blue, the same color as her eyes.

I say, "Brother Enos finds such messages disturbing. If he knew I had been talking to you, I would pay a price."

"Brother Enos sounds like he's got a stick up his butt."

I almost smile, as it sounds like something my mother might say. I tear my eyes from her face and look past her at the ATV. It looks nothing like Nodd's ATV. It is painted camouflage colors, and it has bigger tires.

"Pretty sweet, huh?" Lynna says, following my glance. "It'll do sixty on the road. You could do your whole edge thing in, like, an hour."

I was thinking the same thing. Although such a machine would be unable to negotiate the Mire or the forest above the gorge, it would make the rest of my patrol go quickly.

"You ever drive one?" she asks.

I nod. I have driven Nodd's ATV several times.

"You want to try it?"

"I cannot leave Nodd."

"Not even for a few minutes?" She is amused, and my face grows warm.

"You do not understand," I tell her.

"You're like a prisoner. I think they got you brainwashed."

"I am not brainwashed."

"Prove it." She crosses her arms.

Several things are going through my mind. I know she is attempting to manipulate me, to use my pride to make me do something I know I should not do. But I am also thinking about the long walk ahead of me, and about Sister Ruth embracing Father Grace, and about Tobias, and about the sun on Lynna's hair. In truth, I would like very much to sit upon her machine.

"I don't have to prove anything," I say, but I consider the hole beneath the fence and consider its size. Is there enough space for me to wriggle through? I am not certain.

"Looks kind of tight," Lynna says, echoing my thoughts.

"There is room," I say. I find it strange how I am no longer thinking about the rightness or wrongness of leaving Nodd, but only of how I will do it. I lie down on my back with my head facing the fence and push myself down into the gap. My head and shoulders pass beneath the fence easily, but the pronged bottom of the chain-link catches on my chest. I exhale to flatten my chest, but I remain wedged. I struggle against it for a few seconds, then start to work my way back. Suddenly Lynna is standing above me with one foot on either side of my head. She is wearing cowboy boots. Her feet are so close, I can smell the leather. She grabs the chain-link with her hands and pulls up, giving me a couple of inches of space. I am looking straight up at the crotch of her jeans.

"Come on!" I can hear the effort in her voice. I push with my legs, and a moment later, I pass through the fence, between her legs, and I am out of Nodd.

Lynna brushes her hands on her thighs.

"That wasn't so hard," she says.

I look through the fence, feeling an eerie mix of freedom and fear.

"Come on," she says. "Check out my ride."

The seat of the ATV is warm and foreign between my legs. Peter's ATV is like a small Jeep, with a steering wheel and foot pedals. This ATV has handlebars, and instead of a wide seat designed for two people to ride side by side, it has a single long saddle. I grasp the handgrips and listen as Lynna instructs me. She points out a small lever near my right thumb.

"That's the accelerator. You've got two brakes, here and here. Two forward gears and one reverse. You turn the key to start it, just like a car." She reaches past me and twists the key. The engine snarls to life. My heart is beating rapidly. Brother Peter's ATV is quiet and sedate; this machine feels powerful and alive.

To my surprise, she swings herself onto the seat behind me and shoves her helmet down onto my head. Her thighs are touching me. I am paralyzed with sensation.

"Squeeze the brake and put it in gear," she says over my shoulder, her lips inches from my left ear.

I cannot move. My hands are locked onto the handgrips.

"Are you okay?"

"I'm fine." My voice comes out too high.

"Squeeze the brake lever with your left hand."

I do so.

"Okay, now pop it in gear."

When I do not respond, she reaches past me and pushes

the gearshift lever forward. The machine quivers, and the sound of the idling engine becomes deeper.

"Let go of the brake now. But don't touch the accelerator yet."

I release the pressure on the brake lever; the machine begins to creep forward along the cattle trail, following the fence line.

"Give it a little gas," she says.

I push the accelerator lever with my thumb. The machine jerks forward; my body lurches back against Lynna. My hand clutches the brake lever and the ATV stops abruptly, nearly sending me over the handlebars.

"I'm sorry!" I say. I try to get off the machine, but Lynna grabs my shoulders and shoves me back down onto the seat.

She is laughing.

"It's okay. Just hang on tight and press the accelerator slowly. There's no rush."

It takes a few more tries for me to get a feel for the machine, then suddenly I have it. The power of the engine flows through my hands and legs. The machine becomes an extension of my body, of my soul.

"You got it now," Lynna says.

I lean forward and accelerate down the cattle trail, the fence a chain-link blur to my right, wind tearing at my face, Lynna's arms wrapped tight around my chest, her body pressing against my back. I hear her screaming in my ear but my mind is as open and clear as the Montana sky.

15

It lasts only seconds, that moment of wind and speed and power, before I am overcome by the immensity of what I am doing. I release the accelerator. We coast to a bumpy stop.

Lynna loosens her grip around my middle, reaches past me, and puts the gearshift in neutral.

"You're kind of wild, you know that?" She sets the brake and hops off the ATV.

I am shaking. I fear to look at her. I am ashamed. It is true what Father Grace has long told us. Machines can devour us; they are eaters of souls.

"What's the matter?" Lynna asks.

I climb off the machine and begin walking back up the trail. Seconds later I hear the growl of the machine but I do not look back. The sound grows louder and she is on my right, pacing me.

"Jacob? Are you okay?"

"I must not do this thing," I say.

"What thing?"

I do not answer.

"Just stop for a second," she says.

I stop.

"If you're leaving, you could at least give me back my helmet," she says.

I didn't realize I was still wearing it. I remove the helmet and hold it out to her, looking at the ground. She takes the helmet. I walk quickly to the hole beneath the fence and wriggle beneath it. The bottom of the chain-link catches on my front; I force myself through, tearing my garment.

Lynna is watching me.

"You're kind of weird." she says.

"I have work to do. Thank you for letting me drive your machine." I turn my back and wait for her to leave so that I can repair the gap beneath the fence in peace.

"Jacob . . ." she says. Her voice creeps over my shoulder and hangs there.

I don't say anything. I sense that she is not going to leave. I turn to her, intending to say something that will drive her away. The expression on her face stops me. She looks sad and hurt.

"I'm sorry," I say.

She nods carefully, then ventures a smile. "Are you hungry?"

I think of the food in my backpack. I have not eaten since leaving Menshome.

"I have food," I say.

"Me too. Hang on a sec." She runs to the ATV, opens a compartment behind the seat, and unstraps a small pack from the back. "Catch!" The pack comes sailing over the fence. I catch it. Lynna smiles and claps her hands. "Touchdown!"

I set the pack on the ground. I don't know what a "touchdown" is.

"Why did you do that?" I ask.

In answer, she walks over to the breach and starts to wriggle beneath the fence. The bottom of the chain-link catches on her jacket.

"A little help here?" she says.

"You're not supposed to come in here," I say, but even as I am speaking, I grab the chain-link and pull up, freeing her. A moment later, she is standing beside me.

She looks around and says, "Wow, the grass really is greener on the other side."

"That is because we do not crowd our land with cattle."

She unzips the pack, pulls out a checkered cloth, and spreads it on the grass.

"What are you doing?"

"Making a picnic."

I watch dumbly as she lays out a meal: several plastic tubs

containing unfamiliar foods, a bright-red-and-blue bag of potato chips, and an assortment of candies with wrappers in a rainbow of colors.

"I wasn't sure what you like," she said. "Or even if you'd be here. So I just threw in a bunch of different stuff."

I realize then that she has planned this, and a shiver of fear runs up my body. Is this all a part of some Worldly plot? At the same time, I am flattered and excited.

"What is that?" I ask, pointing at two bottles of orange liquid.

"Pop," she says. "It was the only kind we had."

"Pop . . ." I remember soda pop from when I was little, the tickle and fizz of it going down my throat. Suddenly I am desirous of it, and my decision is made. I think of the food in my pack: soda bread, hard cheese, a seedcake, and a bottle of water. My drab offerings would be an insult to this colorful feast.

I sit down on one end of the checkered cloth as she kneels and opens one of the plastic tubs. It is filled with golden, irregular lumps.

"What is that?" I ask.

She smiles. "Fried chicken. Do you like chicken?"

I nod. Chicken is a familiar food, but I have never had it so prepared. She puts pieces on two paper plates and opens another tub.

"Beans," I say. They are dark brown, swimming in sauce.

She loads the plates with beans, pouring them directly

from the tub. I feel as if I am in a dream. She tears open a bag of potato chips and adds the thin crisps to our plates. I remember potato chips. My mouth is watering. She hands me a plate. I place it on the cloth before me, uncertain how to proceed. She hands me a fork and one of the orange sodas. The bottle is icy cold in my hand. She twists the cap off the other soda; I do the same with mine.

We drink. The soda is excruciatingly sweet. Occasionally, as a special treat, the Archcherubim return from their travels with crates of oranges or other exotic fruits. This soda does not taste much like an orange, but it is very good. I gulp greedily, emptying half the bottle.

"It's good," I say with a gasp.

"You never had pop?"

"Not since I was little." I bite into a piece of chicken. It's crusty and flavorful. The beans are as sweet as the soda, and the potato chips are astonishingly salty, but seductive. I eat quickly, in part because the food is delicious and partly so that I do not have to talk.

"You must be hungry!" she says as I finish what is on my plate. "Do you want more?"

"Please," I say. She gives me more chicken and beans and chips.

"What kind of food do you usually eat?" she asks.

"Just . . . regular food." I think again of the drab food in my pack. "I can show you." I open my pack and unwrap what was to be my lunch. "The seedcake is good." I offer her a piece; she tastes it.

"It's like a granola bar," she says, chewing carefully. "What kind of cheese is that?"

"Cheese. We make it from the milk of our ewes."

She breaks off a small piece, sniffs it, puts it in her mouth. "Kind of gamy," she says. I don't know what she means. "So you guys make all your own food?"

"Mostly."

"Does it get boring?"

"It is what we eat."

"Do you have to work all the time?"

"We work as it is needed. We study. We worship. We hunt. We play."

"What kind of play?"

"A game called chess. Have you heard of it?"

"Chess? Sure, lots of people play chess."

I look at the checkered tablecloth. "We could play chess here. We could use candies for pieces."

Lynna thinks that's funny. I am embarrassed again.

"I'm afraid you'd beat me," she says. "I don't even know the moves."

"I could teach you."

"I'd rather eat the candy than play with it." She tosses me a small brown bag. M&M's, it says. I open it and pour several candies into my palm and stare at them, so smooth and bright. I pick out a blue tablet and bite into it. Sweetness floods my mouth. Lynna is eating a strand of red licorice. I remember red licorice.

She says, "Is it true that you guys are polygamists? Like, the men have a bunch of wives?"

"Father Grace has four wives. Brother Enos has two." I have the feeling this is a dangerous subject. "Most men take one wife only."

"Do you have more than one mom?"

"No."

"Do you have any brothers or sisters?"

"No."

"Are there other teenagers besides you?"

I think of Ruth, and Tobias.

"There are Grace of all ages," I say.

Lynna has many more questions, and soon I find myself talking easily. We sit in the autumn sun and I find myself telling her of Father Grace, and of the Ark that will come.

"You mean you think that some kind of spaceship is going to carry you all away just before the end of the world?" she asks.

"Not a spaceship. The Ark. Father Grace has seen it. It will come from the west."

"Like from Idaho?"

I sense she is making fun of me. I stop talking.

"Sorry," she says, looking serious. "I guess it just seems weird to me."

"It is the Truth."

"When is it supposed to happen? The end of the world."

"Not until the Tree bears sweet fruit and dies."

"Tree?"

"The Tree is why we are here."

"What sort of tree? Ponderosa? Oak?"

"It is just the Tree."

"Every tree is *some* kind of tree."

"I do not think it is a *kind* of tree. It is *the* Tree."

"What kind of fruit does it make?"

"Small round red fruits." I make a circle with my thumb and forefinger.

"Do you eat them?"

"No!" The thought horrifies me.

"I was just asking. So what makes this tree so special?"

I hesitate, as I remember Brother Peter saying that our missionaries do not speak of the Tree to Worldly folk. *It induces them to ridicule,* he said. *They laugh at that which they do not understand.*

I do not want to be laughed at by Lynna, but the Tree is a part of me, and I feel I must tell her something of it.

"Have you read the Bible?" I ask her.

"Some," she says. "I'm not all that churchy."

"But you know the story of Genesis, don't you?"

"That's the part with Adam and Eve, right?"

"Yes! You know that in the Garden of Eden, the Lord placed the Tree of Knowledge, and he commanded Adam and Eve never to eat of it, but they did, and they were banished."

I pause to gauge her reaction. She is not laughing. She nods and says, "Yeah, I know about that."

Encouraged, I continue. "Adam and Eve were sent away,

and the Lord placed Cherubim and the whirling sword at the east of Eden to prevent them from ever returning. And that's where we all came from."

Lynna is looking at me intently.

I lick my lips and say, "The Lord has given us a second chance. Years ago, when Father Grace discovered the Tree, he bought this land. The Tree now grows at the Sacred Heart of Nodd." I am speaking more quickly now, I want to get it out, to share the Good News with her. "It lives that we might create a new Eden around it, a Garden as beautiful as Eden, and only then will the fruit of the Tree grow large and sweet, but still we must not eat of it, and the Tree will die, and the Ark will come with the Archangel Zerachiel at its helm to carry the Grace to the arms of the Lord while all else withers and dies."

"*All* else? You mean like me?"

"Unless you join us," I say.

Lynna's eyes are enormous; she is staring at me as if I am the only thing in all of creation.

Then she laughs.

16

"It is not funny," I say, embarrassed and uncomfortable, as if I have shown her my naked self and been found wanting.

"Sorry," she says. "It's just sort of . . . um . . . *biblical,* I guess. The whole ark thing, and the magic tree."

"It is the Truth."

"When's all this stuff supposed to happen?" she asks.

"Brother Andrew believes it will be soon. The Garden grows more beautiful each spring."

She is shaking her head. I feel her withdrawing. She does not believe. I wonder what she *does* believe, and I realize that I have asked her nothing of herself. I search my mind for a question. All I can think to say is, "What about you?"

The question seems to startle her.

"What *about* me?" she says.

"I mean, what's it like being . . . you?"

"It's okay," she says. "Kind of boring sometimes. I mean, we're just a little operation, thirty-three sections, half of it rock or arroyo. Max says it's too big anyways. Too much work for me and Max and Cal and Chico."

"Who are they?"

"Max is my dad. Chico's a hand. Cal is my asshole uncle." She takes a folding knife from her pocket and opens it. The blade is four inches long, with a wicked hook at the end. She takes an apple from the basket, uses the odd blade to slice it, and offers me half. I take the half apple and set it on the cloth before me.

"Brother Peter has a knife like that," I say. "He uses it to neuter the rams."

"I call it my *Cal*-strating knife," she says, then laughs. "I told Cal I'd use it on him if he ever tried anything."

I don't understand, and then I think I do. A cold, unspeakable lump manifests in my gut.

"He . . . touched you?"

"Nope. He wouldn't dare." She wipes the apple juice from the blade on her jeans and snaps the knife closed with one hand. "He knows I can take care of myself. Cal's actually not such a bad guy when he's sober. Except for being a total lech sometimes. Anyway, it's mostly just the three of us. Max hires in other guys when we need them, but it's seasonal."

"What about your mother?" I ask, although I am afraid I know the answer.

"She died."

That is the answer I was afraid of.

"She got breast cancer when I was eleven. I was twelve when she went." She says it matter-of-factly, but I sense she does not want to talk about it.

"Do you go to school?" I ask.

She shakes her head. "I did until last year when I kind of got in trouble. This year I'm homeschooling. Mostly just my dad making me read boring stuff. I'll take some tests in the spring and get my diploma. It's no big deal."

"You got in trouble?"

"I got caught smoking weed."

"Some of the Archcherubim smoke," I say, thinking of Enos and his pipe.

She laughs. "I bet they don't smoke what *I* was smoking."

I don't know what she is talking about, but I sense that she has sinned mightily. I notice then that the shadow cast by the fence is long, and the sun is low in the sky. I jump to my feet. "I must go."

"So soon?" She looks disappointed.

"I must repair the fence hole. And I have much walking to do." Judging by the sun, I will not get home until after dark. Enos will make inquiries. I am already forming excuses and lies in my mind.

Lynna is gathering up the remains of our meal.

"Give me a minute to pack this up," she says, fitting the empty containers into her pack. "I'll help you fill in the hole."

"Thank you." I pick up a rock and move it over to the

fence. It will take many such stones to fill the gap beneath the chain-link.

She says, "Hey, don't block me in!" She zips her pack shut and starts to wriggle back under the fence. I pull up on the chain-link, and she is through. "Throw me my pack?"

I loft her pack up over the razor wire. She stows it in her ATV, then starts gathering stones. With both of us working from different sides, it takes only a few minutes to fill the gap.

"I think that's enough," I say.

We look at each other through the fence. Her blue-nailed fingers grasp the chain-link.

"It was fun hanging with you," she says.

I am not sure why she says "hanging," but I take her meaning.

"Me too," I say, moving closer. Though we spent much of the afternoon together, we have not touched. Now, with the fence between us, I reach out and twine my fingers in hers.

"I like you," she says, then grins. "Even if you are a super-serious cult boy who never smiles."

I laugh. How long has it been?

"He laughs!" She squeezes my fingers. "He smiles!"

We stand there grinning at each other for a few seconds.

"Let's do this again," she says. "Next, um, *Landay?*"

"Landay after next," I say. "I walk the fence on the second and fourth Landays."

"In two weeks then. About the same time?"

I nod. Our fingers slip apart and the moment is ended. I mount my pack on my shoulders, pick up my shovel and carbine, and set off along the fence. I will miss supper and Babel Hour, but I do not care. My fingertips are buzzing; I can still feel her touch. I hear the burble of the ATV engine. A few seconds later, Lynna is riding parallel to me on the other side. She waves. I wave back. We continue along the fence, keeping each other company for nearly a mile, until the fence line dips down to enter the northeast bowl, a wooded area where her machine cannot go. With a final wave, she veers off and accelerates. I stop and watch her until the ATV is out of sight.

17

I am bubbling inside. I have touched a girl. My fingers tingle with memory, and I feel something else deep inside. I have stepped outside the Grace. Father Grace has taken Ruth from me, but I have touched a girl. I feel triumph, a sense of power, as I enter the woods. The hill behind me eclipses the sun, but a lightness sustains me as I move down the shadowed path into the quiet murk of the forest.

I quicken my pace. The sun will set within the hour. I still have five miles of fence to patrol, but the walking will be easy. Each impact of my feet hitting the trail joggles the images in my mind.

Lynna. Ruth. Father Grace.

The trees seem to lean in on me. My feet hit the packed earth like the chuffing of a motor.

Will. Tobias.

I wish I could tell them what I have done, but it must remain a secret. I have a secret.

The Tree. Babel Hour.

I will not regret missing Babel Hour. But there will be questions. I imagine myself sitting before Enos, telling him more lies.

Enos. My father. Von.

Suddenly I am staggering beneath the onus of my sins. What have I done? There is no way I can meet with Lynna again. My stomach churns with the weight of strange Worldly foods. I fear I will vomit them up, but I keep moving and the moment passes.

I start to run. The trail steepens; the pack straps hammer my shoulders. I am not even looking at the fence. I run until the thoughts in my head become a blur and the pain in my legs and shoulders is all that occupies me. For a few seconds, the physical pain provides me with mental peace. I lengthen my stride, and my foot comes down on an exposed root, turning it in, sending me sprawling headfirst. The carbine and shovel go flying, and the pack slams into my back as I hit the hard earth. I know at once that something bad has happened, even before the pain rockets from my ankle up my right leg.

I do not move. I know it will hurt. My leg feels hot. I imagine a broken bone, jutting out through the skin of my ankle. I wonder if I will be able to move at all or if I will simply lie there until I die. No, not die. Enos will send out searchers.

Carefully I turn onto my back. The pain is less than I feared. I sit up and carefully unlace my boot. I peel back the sock. My skin is unbroken, but my ankle is swelling rapidly. I try to move it. It hurts, but not terribly. Maybe it is just a sprain. I grab a nearby birch sapling and stand up using my good leg. The forest whirls around me. I hang tight to the sapling until the dizziness passes, then test the injured ankle with some weight. It feels wrong, but it doesn't hurt. I take a step. My ankle explodes with pain; I gasp and grab the sapling again. I lower myself to the ground and wait for the trees to stop spinning.

Using the small saw in my pack, I cut down the little sapling that served me so well and use the fence-repair tools in my pack to fashion it into a sort of crutch. I hobble around for several steps to test it. It will be slow going, but at least I can move. My fear of being stranded leaves me, to be replaced with a sense of satisfaction. By the most direct route, the Village is less than two miles distant. I am confident I can make it back, even if I have to crawl.

I gather my shovel and carbine, fasten them to my pack, and begin the long journey home. At least I will not be blamed for shirking my duty. My injury will tell its own lies about why I will be arriving so late.

It is a very long walk. I follow the fence line toward the road that will take me home, one lurching step at a time. The pain from my ankle comes and goes in dizzying waves, and the failing light makes the footing treacherous. Twice I fall and lie on the trail, thinking it might be best to simply build a fire and wait for help. It cannot be long before Brother Enos sends out search parties. But both times I get up and keep moving.

As I come up out of the woods and onto the north ridge, the last glimmer of sunset has come and gone, and I have only completed a small part of my journey. With two good legs, I could reach the Village within half an hour, but on this night I estimate it will take another three hours of hobbling.

By the time I reach the North Road, my armpit is rubbed raw from the rough crossbar of the crutch, my ankle is a throbbing melon hanging off the end of my leg, and it is pitch-dark. Still a mile to go, but now that I am on the road the walking will be easier.

I leave the pack, the shovel, and my carbine by the side of the road. Brother Peter can pick them up later in his ATV. I continue on. All thoughts of the Worldly girl have left me. I think only of the next step. I am cold. The warmth left with the sun, and I can see my breath, but I am sweating. Icy sweat runs down my face onto my neck. My eyes are fixed on the dirt surface of the road a few steps in front of me. My universe is reduced to a few square cubits. I attempt to pray, but the prayers I know so well are jumbled and meaningless. I take this as a sign that Zerachiel will not help me now. I have touched a girl. I have only this crude crutch, and my will, to carry me home.

Something compels me to raise my head, and I see a ghostly blur standing on the road a few dozen cubits ahead. I stop and try to make it out. At first I think I am looking at one of our flock, a sheep that has found a breach in the fence. But its shape is wrong. This is no sheep.

It is the wolf.

I reach for my carbine, but it is not there. I left it with my pack, back by the gate. I look around, but see no other wolves. A lone wolf is not likely to attack, I tell myself.

The wolf is moving, coming toward me slowly.

"Go away!" I wave my crutch and almost fall down. I catch myself. Falling would be bad. To a wolf, revealing myself to be crippled would be an invitation to dinner.

The wolf stops and sits down about twenty paces away. I can make out some of the details of its face. I feel in my pocket for my folding knife. A three-inch blade is small defense against a mouthful of canine teeth, but it is all I have.

"I'll hurt you," I say.

The wolf tips its head. I sense it is amused.

"You don't belong here. Go!"

The wolf yawns.

I don't know what else to do, so I start moving toward him. The wolf stands and trots off to the side and into the field bordering the road. I keep moving. The wolf, less than a stone's throw away, flanks me on my left. From time to time, it pulls ahead, then stops and waits for me to catch up. I go back and forth between watching the road surface in front of me and checking on the wolf. After perhaps ten minutes of this, the creature is gone. I stop and turn in a circle. The wolf has vanished. It could be lying low in the grasses. At any moment it might come leaping out of the blackness to tear open my throat. I keep moving, looking from the road ahead to the left, to the right, and every two steps turning to look behind. It is excruciatingly slow going. I imagine the wolf laughing at me from the darkness.

Time passes. The Village grows closer. I come to think that the wolf is truly gone, that it has gone off in search of more familiar prey. In any case, I am too exhausted to keep stopping and looking behind me. It occurs to me that the wolf may have been an avatar of Zerachiel, or of some dark lord. Or it may have been a hallucination, a dream, a waking nightmare. Is it possible to walk and dream at the same time? I cannot be certain. Not that it matters. I can only keep moving.

An eternity later, I see the faint glow of lights ahead. I can make out the shape of the Tower, a black cutout in the starry sky. I am in much pain, but it is easier to bear now that the Village is in sight. Only a few hundred more steps. I imagine myself in my mother's arms.

The Hall of Enoch is ablaze with lights. It is unusual for it to be lit up so late at night. It takes me another eternity to limp up the walkway to the entrance. I push through the doors.

All the men of Nodd are gathered around the long table at the side of the room. I stand at the back of the hall, unnoticed.

". . . in eighteen days they will come," Enos is saying. "The politicians, the lawyers, the misguided, the heathens, the apostates, the degenerate—they come to Nodd to undo us with their lies and their hatred. We must gird ourselves. They must see us not as a threat, but as a people strong, determined, and righteous. Any sign of discontent will be reason for them to pry further into our affairs. We must present ourselves in the best possible light."

"What of the boy?" asks Brother John.

For a moment I think he is talking about me, but Enos says, "Tobias is staying in Gracehome at present. Father Grace is working with him day and night. The boy will be ready by the time his uncle arrives."

"And Brother Von?"

"Father Grace does not want Von disturbed by Worldly influences. He will be confined to the catacombs. We must present ourselves as cordial but strong. We will offer them our best food; we will allow them access to all areas save the Sacred Heart and the catacombs. We do not want them to perceive us as a threat, but at the same time we must show them that we are prepared to defend our rights."

"The women will want to know how many are coming," says Brother Peter.

"As many as *gabble*," Enos says, "and *dabble babble gubba.*"

I shake my head. Is he speaking in tongues? My ears are buzzing. The floor seems to tilt. I clutch my crutch with both hands. One of the other men speaks meaningless noises that rattle against my ears. They are talking gibberish, and the air in the room is hot and moist and my head is floating. I open my mouth and a sound comes out, their faces turn toward me, and the floor rises to smite my face.

18

My mother's hand.

I know it is my mother's hand; her cool palm cups my forehead in that old familiar way. I feel safe, although I know not where I am, nor how I have come to be here.

"Jacob." My mother's voice. I open my eyes. My mother's face, creased with worry, but smiling.

"Mom." I have not called her Mom in years. She is Sister Elena Grace.

I look past her. I am in the infirmary, just off the nursery. I hear Sister Fara's infant daughter, Mariah, crying on the other side of the wall.

"You have had quite an ordeal," my mother says. "You slept the night and much of the day away."

I raise my head and look down my blanketed body. My right leg is propped up, my heavily bandaged ankle sticking out from beneath the sheets.

"Is it broken?" I ask.

"Brother Samuel believes it is a bad sprain, with possibly a minor fracture. You will not be patrolling the fence anytime soon."

Yesterday comes rushing back at me. My mother leans closer. "Are you all right?"

"I am fine," I say. And I *am* fine. The decision of whether I should again meet with the Worldly girl is taken from me. It was Zerachiel who put that tree root on the path, where He knew I would fall and injure myself. The Lord has reached out His Hand to punish me for my transgressions, while at the same time saving me from myself.

"What happened, dear Jacob?"

"It was my own clumsiness. I tripped and fell."

She smiles. "You must have stopped the fall with your face."

I reach up a hand and feel my nose. It is tender. I would ask for a mirror, but that would be self-seeking and vain.

"That must have happened after I got back."

"Yes, Brother Samuel said you passed out and fell during their meeting. Are you well enough to speak with Brother Enos? He has been asking after you."

I nod.

My mother leaves, and I am left alone to wonder why my father has not come to see his son, who was conceived in sin. After a time, my thoughts wander beyond the borders of Nodd, and I think of Lynna. I am thinking of her when Brother Enos glides into the room to stand at the foot of my pallet.

"Brother Jacob. You look well, thanks be to the Lord."

"And to Zerachiel's hand on my back," I say. My heart is pounding; it always seems to me that Enos can sense my thoughts.

"How did you injure yourself?" he asks.

"A tree root on the path. Where the fence line runs through the North Wood. I was careless."

"Indeed. You must be more cautious in the future. What of your pack and your rifle?"

I tell him where I left them.

"I will send Gregory to fetch them. And what of the fence repair with which you were charged?"

"It was a small breach. A marmot, perhaps. It is repaired."

Enos nods, satisfied.

"I hope the searchers were not out too late looking for me," I say.

Enos gives a faint shrug. "We had not yet dispatched them. In truth, you were not missed, with all that is happening."

I feel a sense of betrayal. Had I been injured more seriously I might have lain there all through the night.

"And what is happening?" I ask.

"In seventeen days, the World is coming to Nodd."

* * *

That afternoon, Brother Wallace arrives with a pair of crutches, freshly made. Wallace does beautiful work. The crutches are made of fine ash, padded with leather and fleece. I use them to lift myself up off the pallet. Wallace looks at me critically as I stand before him on three legs.

"If they are too long, I can shorten them," he says.

"They are perfect," I say. "I thank you."

He frowns. "Sit." He takes the crutches from me and adjusts the handgrips. "Try now." He hands them back to me.

I walk back and forth across the room.

"Even better," I say.

He nods, believing me this time.

"Brother Enos tells me we have many visitors coming," I say.

"He tells me that as well," Wallace says sourly. "I have many chairs to build."

With that, he turns and leaves.

19

Over the next days, Nodd becomes a hive of activity. Worldly folk will be coming with their wicked ways and sinful thoughts, and that frightens us, but at the same time, we are excited to show them the paradise we have built. Jerome and Luke put a fresh coat of paint on the North Gate, Brother Peter regrades the road, and Brother John distributes newly made clothing to everyone. Even Elder Abraham, who disdains vanity in all its forms, has consented to have his beard combed.

I have not seen Tobias. I am told he is staying in Gracehome, taking instruction from Father Grace, preparing for the visitation. I fear that when I see him again, Tobias will not be the Tobias I know.

I have been assigned whatever small tasks lie within my capabilities: assisting Brother Samuel in the infirmary, filing papers for Brother Caleb, helping in the laundry, and so forth. My hands are kept busy as my ankle heals and my mind roams. I am alone in the laundry one day, folding and bundling clean clothing destined for Menshome, when I hear my mother's voice.

"You have a sure hand with those trousers, Brother." It is her teasing voice. I am not surprised to find a smile upon her face.

"It is not so difficult," I say. "Even a Sister could do it."

She laughs. "I will never understand how laundry became women's work. Perhaps, after the Fall, Eve said to Adam, 'I will wash your fig leaf if you will till the soil.'" As is often the case, my mother's words verge upon blasphemy without quite crossing the line.

"If so, Adam made a poor bargain," I say.

She laughs again and begins smoothing and folding items from the pile of clean clothing. Her movements are swift and deft; I feel clumsy by comparison. As we work, she talks. "It's nice to see everyone working together to impress our Worldly visitors. This dreaded visitation might turn out to be a good thing for all of us. Nodd is like a sixteen-year-old girl getting ready for her first prom," she says.

I don't know what a prom is, and I am embarrassed to ask. I finish tying a bundle of clean trousers and slide them down the table.

"Brother Samuel tells me your ankle is healing well," she says.

"It is much better," I say.

"Your father worries about you."

A spark of anger flares in my breast. "He did not visit me when I was abed."

My mother touches me lightly, fingertips brushing my arm. "He did, Jacob. He was with you while you were dreaming. We sat together by your bedside and prayed for you all through the night. He had to leave for Helena that morning to meet with the congressman who will be visiting us. That is the only reason he was not with you when you awakened."

I feel the sting of moisture in my eyes and look quickly away.

"He is in Omaha now. Brother Joseph and Sister Anna have left the Grace. Your father is closing the Omaha ministry. He will be home soon."

I am surprised to hear this. I met Joseph and Anna only once, when they came to Nodd to view the Garden and take counsel with Father Grace. They seemed very devout; it is hard for me to imagine them becoming apostates.

"People come, people go," my mother says. "It is their nature. But your father will be back in time for the visitation. He loves you, Jacob."

I clear my throat, but I have nothing to say. My mother perceives my shame; her fingertips brush my arm again and she leaves me to my task.

By second Landay, I am able to put some weight on my ankle and get about using only a single crutch, but it will be many more weeks before I am able to resume my edge-walking duties. Gregory walks the fence in my place. I think of Lynna. Will she be there, waiting? Will she call out to Gregory, mistaking him for me? Will she offer him potato chips and orange soda?

That night, after Gregory returns from his walk, I sit with him at supper and ask him about his day.

"I walked," he says shortly. "What do you think? There is the fence. There are marmots and coyotes and ravens. I walked, and now the day is gone. Were it not for your clumsiness I would not now be sore and exhausted."

"Your walk was uneventful, then?"

"I didn't fall and twist my ankle," he says with an accusing glare. "Though you can be sure I kept a sharp lookout for wayward roots seeking to leap out and trip me."

"Did you see any of the Rocking K folk?"

"One watched me from his machine as I passed. I ignored him."

Lynna, I think. If she had been wearing her helmet, Gregory would not know her for a girl. I wonder what she thought, seeing him instead of me.

"Why do you ask?" He gives me a sideways look.

"I was wondering if any of them would be coming to the visitation," I say.

Gregory shrugs and says, "Rumors are flying like mad locusts. It would not surprise me if the Archangel Zerachiel himself were to show up, along with Enoch and all his wives."

It is a borderline blasphemous thing to say, but he is right. Rumors about the impending visit are rife; it is hard to know what to believe. Will says he heard from Brother John that they are coming with armed soldiers to take our women, while Samuel frets that Worldly doctors will wish to examine his medical credentials. Sister Dalva, who is in charge of the kitchens, is in a frenzy over how to prepare a feast for an unknown number of people.

Still, I credit what I have heard from Brother Enos, who visited the kitchens a few days ago. I had been put to work shelling beans and overheard him telling Dalva to expect at least a dozen, but not more than two dozen guests.

"Well?" Dalva crossed her arms. "What is it to be, then? Twelve or twenty-four?"

"It is uncertain," Enos told her. "We know that Congressman Raney will be coming from Helena, along with several of his staff. The mayor of West Fork will be here, and the Landreau County sheriff, and Father Gerard from Saint Margaret's, and the superintendent of the West Fork schools, and a reporter from the newspaper. We have extended invitations to our neighbors as well."

We have only two adjacent neighbors: the Fort Landreau Indian Reservation and the Rocking K Ranch.

"Our visitors will include both men and women, but you need not set up separate dining areas."

"I don't understand," Sister Dalva said. It was clear from her expression that she understood perfectly but did not like what she was hearing.

Enos pretended to not notice the scowl on Dalva's features.

"We will serve a midday supper in the Hall of Enoch. The Archcherubim, Elders, and their wives will join them. We will not be dividing according to gender, as the Worldly folk are not accustomed to dining apart. Our goal on this day is to make them as comfortable as possible."

I think I understand. It is to be Babel Hour gone mad.

The day before the visitation, I am cleaning shelves in the infirmary when I sense someone watching me. Thinking it is Brother Samuel, I redouble my efforts.

"I heard you injured yourself, Brother."

I turn to find Tobias standing behind me.

"Tobias! It is good to see you!" He is different. His face is pale from his time in the Pit, and his scalp has been shorn, a symbol of expiation. When his hair grows back, its length will signify the days of his righteousness.

"I am glad to see you as well, Brother." He speaks slowly, spacing out his words. I peer closely at him and I am relieved to see that, unlike Brother Von, Tobias does not bear the scars of exorcism beneath his brow.

"Are you well?" I ask.

"Father Grace has explained much to me. I see now that I was wrong, and I have come to apologize to you."

"To me? For what?"

"For leading you astray. Forgive me, Brother."

I wonder at the change he has undergone. Could he be drugged? I do not think so, for his eyes would not then be so focused. He has spent weeks with the voice of Father Grace in his ears. We have all felt the relentless power of that voice; I cannot imagine it for hours and days on end.

"I should beg *your* forgiveness," I say. "The error was mine."

Tobias gives me a flat, expressionless stare, then nods. "I do forgive you, and I go now to the Heart to pray for you. Father Grace suggests that I speak the Arbor Prayer two score times daily."

"That is a lot of praying. Your knees must be getting sore."

"The time goes quickly."

"Will you be returning to Menshome?"

"Father Grace wishes me to remain in Gracehome for now."

"I hear your uncle will be visiting soon."

"Yes. It will be good to see him."

We stand there awkwardly. I do not know what to say. I am happy that Tobias has been released and that he has embraced the ways of the Grace, but I miss that which is missing.

"This afternoon I go to help Brother Peter cut thistles," Tobias says.

The invasive Canada thistles are Brother Peter's obsession. Every fall he cuts them back and poisons their roots with a powerful herbicide. Despite his efforts, each year there seem to be more.

"A task without end," I say.

"It will end with the Coming," Tobias says.

"Brother Tobias!" Brother Samuel is glowering in the doorway. "What do you do here?"

Tobias ducks his head. "Apologies, Brother. I have not seen Jacob since before his accident. I came to wish him well."

"As you can see, he is busy," Samuel says. "Have you no chores of your own?"

"I do. My apologies, Brother." Tobias leaves the infirmary, head down.

"I wonder at that one," says Brother Samuel, looking after him.

The day of the visitation, I am put to work in the garage helping Brother Taylor clean and ready our two Jeeps and the ATV, as Brother Peter plans to take our visitors on a tour of our outer fields and pastures and wants nothing to go wrong. Brother Samuel has fashioned a new brace for my ankle, and I am able to hobble about using only a cane.

Brother Taylor is one of my favorite people to work with. He says little, but he is always friendly, knowledgeable, and patient. He puts me to work cleaning the interiors of the Jeeps. I am running a damp cloth over the dashboard of the green Jeep when Taylor says, "I was coming up the North Road a few days back when I saw what was either the biggest coyote ever, or a wolf. Might have been the same one you spotted last winter."

I am surprised and glad to hear that someone else had spotted the wolf in Nodd. I had begun to think that I had imagined it.

"I saw it too, also along the North Road," I say. "The beast paced me as I walked along the road the night I was injured."

"It was not aggressive?"

"It seemed more curious than anything."

"Wolves are smart," Taylor says. "Smarter than people in some ways."

"How do you know about wolves?" I ask.

"I know dogs, and a dog is but a wolf with some of the wild taken out. Back in the before days, I had a kennel. Wish we had a few dogs here, but Father Grace, he don't like them. Never understood why. Onan, he'd do better if he had a dog."

Onan is Taylor's seven-year-old son, a shy boy who takes more than his share of teasing from the other children. Taylor often lets his son help him in the garage. He is as patient and kind with Onan as he is with me. I have envied the boy at times.

"I had a dog," I say.

"Did you? What was its name?"

"Spots." I haven't thought about Spots in a long time.

"That's a good dog name. I suppose you had to give him away when you and your folks moved here."

"I suppose so," I say. "I don't remember."

"That is harsh. A boy should not have to give up his dog."

It sounds perfectly natural and innocent, what Brother Taylor is saying, but as always it is unsettling to hear Father Grace's judgment questioned.

I do not reply. Taylor goes silently about his work, as do I.

Minutes later, we hear the sound of an approaching vehicle. Taylor and I step outside the garage to watch as a shiny silver SUV comes into view.

"That's a Cadillac Escalade," Taylor says. He knows the names of many cars.

Elder Abraham, Brother Enos, and my father have gathered before the Hall of Enoch to greet our visitors. Three men and a woman step out of the SUV. The men are wearing dark suits. The woman is wearing a blue dress with a matching jacket.

I immediately identify the tallest man as Congressman Raney. He wears his gray hair like a helmet and stands with his chest thrust out and his bright-white teeth bared, looking over his surroundings as if surveying his own personal domain. Already I do not like him.

Three more vehicles are coming up the road: two SUVs and a pickup truck.

"Jacob," Taylor says, "finish your task. There will be time to gawk later."

Reluctantly I limp back into the garage and continue wiping down the Jeeps.

I finish quickly. By the time I get back outside, our visitors are being guided into the Hall of Enoch. I see a man whose collar identifies him as the priest, and a man wearing a two-tone brown uniform and a handgun at his hip. He must be the sheriff. The others are dressed in various combinations of colorful clothing. I catch a glimpse of a light-haired young woman wearing a denim jacket. I only see her from the back as she enters the hall, but her hair is exactly the right color. My pulse begins to pound in my throat.

"Brother Jacob!" It is Sister Naomi, coming around from the back of the hall. "When you are finished here, Sister Dalva requests your help with the food service."

I look at Taylor, who quickly inspects my work and pronounces it good.

"Go," he says.

Eagerly, I comply.

20

I enter the Hall of Enoch through the back. Several women are bustling about, setting out stacks of plates and bowls on the serving tables. Dalva looks askance at my cane.

"With that leg, you will be of little use," she says.

"He needs no leg to fill bowls," Naomi says.

I glance out through the archway into the hall proper, where the chairs have been arranged around several long tables. Our visitors are seated, along with the Elders, the Archcherubim, and most of the Higher Cherubim. Several of the married Sisters are there as well. All together there are about forty people seated at four long tables, men and women mixed haphazardly. Beryl and Angela are moving along the tables offering herbal tea and water. I can't see everybody from where I'm standing. I move closer to the archway. The rest of the hall comes into view, and I see Lynna seated beside a ruddy, large-featured man with a clay-colored felt hat tipped back on his head. Facing him is a black-haired man wearing a similar hat, but his is set level on his head, and it has a band of polished silver disks. I cannot see his face.

"Well, Brother?" Naomi says. "Can you help ladle soup, or would you rather stand and gawk?"

"I can ladle," I say. She sets me up at one of the serving tables with stacks of shallow bowls and a steel kettle filled with thick corn-and-leek chowder.

As I fill the bowls, they are whisked away by the Sisters and carried out into the hall. The smell of the chowder should be making me hungry, but my stomach is unsettled. As I fill each bowl, I wonder if it will go to Lynna.

Sisters Louise and Rebecca show up carrying between them a kettle of lamb stew so enormous that I am certain it contains an entire sheep. More bowls are filled; the stew is presented with small loaves of seed bread. The service goes quickly. Although I cannot hear what they are talking about in the hall, I sense that it is both formal and awkward. The Worldly folk are here to learn about us, to judge us. Father Grace says that they fear us and would destroy us, but what I feel most is their curiosity.

When the stew is eaten, our guests are presented with trays of pastries and sweet huckleberry tea. The women must have used every dried huckleberry in our larders to make so much tea. Naomi has run out of things for me to do, so I find a place to stand where I am out of the way but can see into the hall.

I am certain the man sitting to Lynna's right is Max Evert, her father. His features are large and coarsened by a lifetime of sun and wind, but he has her eyes. He has the same way of holding his head. He says something to the black-haired man sitting across from him. The man laughs and turns his head slightly so that I can see his face, and I realize with a start that he is one of the dark-skinned Lamanites from the Fort Landreau Indian Reservation.

My father and Brother Enos are moving through the hall, stopping at each table to visit. My father's face is contorted into a smile, an expression wholly unnatural on him. Father Grace has not yet made an appearance. Nor has Tobias.

Tobias's mother and sister are sitting with a heavy-set, pink-faced man with sandy, reddish hair. He is wearing a dark-blue jacket over a shirt that is the same color as his face. I'm guessing he is Tobias's uncle. I wonder whether Tobias will be allowed to speak to him.

Congressman Raney and his group are seated at the center table with Elder Seth. Enos approaches them and exchanges a few words with the congressman, then moves to the table where Lynna is sitting.

I fear that he might ask her about the note she left on the fence, but Enos ignores Lynna and speaks to her father and to the Lamanite. While they are talking, Lynna sees me and she waves. To my considerable relief, Enos does not notice, but Lynna's father looks sharply in my direction. I step back out of their view.

Soon the meal is over and people are rising from their chairs. Brother Peter has arranged to take our visitors on a tour of the High Meadow, though I do not know why these Worldly folk would want to look at sheep and grasses.

Congressman Raney and his companions remain seated. They are joined by Enos and my father, one sitting to either side of the congressman. The rest of the visitors, including Lynna and her father, file out of the hall. When they have left, Enos draws a manila envelope from within his robe and places it on the table. The congressman glances at it, then turns away from Enos and engages my father in conversation. One of the congressman's aides slides the envelope off the table and slips it into his small leather briefcase. The moment the envelope is out of sight, the congressman turns back to Enos and smiles.

I sense that something significant has just occurred, but I am not sure what.

Behind me, the women fall silent. I turn to see Father Grace coming in through the back entrance. I go rigid with astonishment. He is not wearing his usual robe but rather a Worldly suit of smooth beige fabric. His beard has been neatly trimmed, his hair is tied back, and he has covered his blasted eye with a patch the same color as his suit. This must be the face he shows to the World, the Father Grace that Tobias met in Colorado Springs.

With him is his eldest wife, Marianne, who is dressed

148

normally. I look past them expecting to see the other wives, but it is only the two of them. They enter the front of the hall, and Father Grace greets the congressman as an old friend, clasping his hand with both hands and smiling a broad smile such as I have never seen on him. The congressman returns the smile and introduces him to his aides. Father Grace introduces Marianne. I feel light-headed to see so much smiling. Even my father and Enos are showing their teeth.

"Brother, you are in the way." Sister Naomi, carrying an armload of dishes, is glaring at me.

"Apologies, Sister." I take the opportunity to slip out through the back entrance. I follow the walkway along the outside of the Hall of Enoch, leaning hard on my cane. My ankle is throbbing after standing for so long. The visitors who left the hall are climbing into the Jeeps, one of the SUVs, and Peter's ATV. I do not see Lynna.

As the vehicles pull out and head north along the High Meadow Road, I hear laughter coming from around the corner. It sounds like Lynna. I move forward and peer past the buttress. Lynna is standing in the shadow of the hedge, near the east entrance to the Sacred Heart. Tobias stands before her, hip cocked, holding a bucket in one hand, grinning. He says something in a low voice. Lynna laughs and pushes her hair behind her ear. I feel myself growing angry.

Tobias says something else, serious now. Lynna's eyes widen and she leans toward him. Tobias points toward the Tower. Lynna shakes her head and replies. I think she is saying "No way!"

He points at the bag she is carrying over her shoulder. Lynna opens the bag, comes out with a pack of cigarettes, and shakes one out. Tobias sets the bucket at his feet and takes a cigarette. Lynna then takes one for herself and lights them both.

I step out from behind the buttress. Lynna sees me and waves. Tobias looks over. His face freezes. I limp toward them.

"Jacob!" Lynna calls out.

I stare at her stupidly. She is wearing jeans that are tight around the hips but loose in the legs, a pair of pointy boots, and an open denim jacket over a black shirt with red printing across the front. I can't see all of the letters because her jacket covers part of them.

Tobias gives me a bland look. "Brother Jacob," he says. He takes a puff from his cigarette.

I stare back at him, furious. This is the old Tobias. He has been acting this whole time. Lying to me. I believed that he had repented, and now I feel foolish.

"So you guys know each other?" Tobias says.

"Sure," Lynna says. "Me and Jacob are old buds." She puffs self-consciously on her cigarette.

I still do not trust myself to speak. A tendril of smoke from Tobias's cigarette snakes toward me. I slash through the smoke with my cane.

Tobias flinches. "Whoa!" he says. "You're dangerous with that thing."

I glare at him.

"What happened to you?" Lynna asks, looking at my ankle brace.

"Nothing," I say.

"Doesn't look like nothing. Seriously, did you break something?"

"I fractured my ankle." We look at each other for what feels like a long time, but it can only be seconds. "What are you doing here?"

"My dad wanted to come to see the cult." She laughs. "I mean, since we're neighbors. You know?"

"Of course I know!"

She gives me a puzzled look. "It's just an expression. Anyway, I asked him if I could come. Because you didn't show up Tuesday like you said." She points with her cigarette at my ankle. "I guess you got an excuse."

Tobias, looking back and forth between Lynna and me, says, "So that's what you do when you're supposed to be patrolling the fence? You guys hook up?"

I don't know what he means by "hook up."

"Tobias was just telling me he's being held prisoner here," Lynna says.

"No one is a prisoner here," I say.

"Oh yeah?" Tobias's face darkens. "What do you call it when you lock a guy up in a dungeon for a week?"

"You are not locked up now," I say.

"You really lock people in *dungeons?*" Lynna says to me.

"We have no dungeons," I tell her. "Tobias was secluded

151

for a few days because he became violent and injured Brother Will."

"I got in a *fight* because you took all my *stuff*," Tobias says, growing angry.

"*I* didn't take anything. And neither did Will."

He sets his jaw and clenches his fists, and for a moment, I fear he will become violent again, but an instant later he relaxes and opens his hands.

"Well, Enos did, or somebody. It doesn't matter. Just living here is like being in prison. Nothing to do except work and pray. No phones, no TV, can't even get online. And since they stole my iPod I'm suffering from, like, terminal music deprivation."

"Wow," says Lynna. "You guys should come over sometime. I got like a thousand songs off the Internet." She says it as if it is nothing. As if we could just stroll blithely out of Nodd to inflict Worldly music upon our souls.

"Where do you live?" Tobias asks.

"Three miles that way." She points north. "Four if you take the road. Seriously, you guys should come over."

"I would in a second," Tobias says. "But I'm out of here."

"Out of where?"

"Out of *here*. Enos is meeting with me and my uncle later. I'm going to Denver with him."

The thought of leaving Nodd for the chaos and evil of the World seems insane, but I am not surprised. "You will not be missed by all," I say, thinking of Will.

Women's voices are approaching from the hall.

"We must not be seen," I say.

Tobias laughs. "Right, because we'll all get tossed in the dungeon." Tobias picks up his bucket. I see it is empty, but I get a whiff of a strong chemical odor. My mouth opens to ask him what was in it, but he is already walking away from us, toward Menshome. He rounds the corner of the hedge and is gone.

The women are getting close. In a moment they will see us. Without thinking, I grab Lynna's hand. Ignoring the twinges from my ankle, I pull her awkwardly along the hedge that surrounds the Sacred Heart. I don't know what will happen if we are seen together, and I do not wish to find out.

Lynna says, "You're acting really weird, Jacob. If they see us I'll just tell them I got lost and you found me."

"You will not be believed," I say. My body acts before my mind can stop it. I push through the iron gate and we enter the Sacred Heart. I realize I am still holding Lynna's hand; I let go as if it is burning me.

Seconds later, the group of women passes by, chattering and oblivious. A moment later there is silence.

We are alone in the Sacred Heart.

21

"It's pretty in here," Lynna says, looking around.

I am rendered speechless by what I have done, bringing a Worldly girl into this most holy of places. The Tree is basking in the autumn sunlight, soaking up Heaven's radiance in preparation for winter. I half expect to be struck down by a bolt of lightning from the clear blue sky.

"Is that a fish pond?" Lynna dances across the cobblestones past the Tree, hardly looking at it, and stops at the lip of the pond. A large bright-orange koi breaches the surface, sending out a radiance of ripples. "They're beautiful!" She grins at me, and she is beautiful, too. "What are you staring at?"

"You," I say, because it is true.

She looks quickly away, her cheeks coloring. I hope I have not embarrassed her. Her eyes move to the flower beds, then to the praying wall that surrounds the Tree, and finally to the Tree itself.

"What's with the wall?" she asks.

"It is the praying wall. It protects the Tree."

"The tree? That's the special tree you were telling me about?"

I nod.

She narrows her eyes at the Tree, looking doubtful.

"This is the tree you guys worship?"

"We are not pagans," I say. "We do not *worship* the Tree."

"But it's this special holy tree, right?"

"It is the Tree."

Lynna shakes her head. "I got to admit, it's the biggest crab I ever seen."

"Crab?"

Before I can stop her, she hops over the low wall, reaches up, and plucks a fruit from a branchlet. I gape at her helplessly. I would be no less astonished if she had sprouted horns and a tail.

She holds up the fruit. "See? Crabapple. They're too bitter to just eat, but you can make good jelly out of them."

"Come out of there!" I am almost shouting.

"Why?"

I lower my voice. "You can't be in there. Please!" It is all I can do not to clamber over the wall myself and drag her out.

She shrugs, tosses the fruit over her shoulder, and hops back over the wall.

"I don't see what the big deal is. We got a crabapple at home."

I am speechless. My heart is pounding, and I am dizzy. The Sacred Heart whirls around me. I think I may be sick.

"Are you okay?" she says.

I sink to the ground and lean back against the wall and squeeze my eyes closed. The Lord is testing me. It is the same test that Adam failed in the First Garden. This can't be happening, not here before the Lord and Zerachiel and the Tree and all the Grace. A nose-tingling chemical odor hangs in the air. Is it the smell of brimstone?

I force my eyes to open. Lynna's face hovers before me. I imagine her pushing a fruit into my mouth, forcing it down my throat, and I jab at her with my cane.

"Hey!" She jumps back. "Did you just try to hit me?"

"Do not touch me," I hear myself say.

"Are you sure you're okay?"

I am not okay. Everything is wrong. My breath is coming shallow and fast, and I am sure something terrible is about to happen.

"Jacob?"

She is squatting before me. The faint crease between her eyebrows deepens as she stares intently into my face. I close my eyes and see flames; I see her dragging me with her into the pit of Hell. I see my own flesh blackened and flaking, and the hard, pitiless face of Zerachiel receding as I fall. I see the faces of my father, my mother, Father Grace—

"Jacob! Breathe!"

Her voice pierces the curtains of my vision and pulls me back. I take a shuddering breath; Lynna's face swims into focus.

"I have damned us both," I tell her. My voice sounds as if it is coming from miles away.

Her expression moves from confusion and concern toward anger.

"Why? Because I picked a crabapple?" She makes a sputtering sound with her lips. "Look above you! You think this tree—or God, or whatever—is going to miss one sour little nubbin?"

I tip my head back and look up at the uncountable fruits supported by the branches of the Tree. I know I should not listen to her, that she is only trying to lead me deeper into sin, but for a moment, I let myself hope that there is truth in what she says. It was such a small fruit, and one among so many . . .

"Besides," she says, "it's not like I'm going to tell anybody."

"Zerachiel knows," I say.

"Zerachiel's another god, right? Like the tree?"

The utter foolishness of her question makes it impossible to answer. I shake my head helplessly.

She must sense my frustration. Her face softens and she says, "Sorry. I suppose from your point of view I'm some sort of ignorant savage."

"You have read some of the Bible," I say. "You are no Lamanite."

"I'm no what?"

"Lamanite. Like the man who was sitting with you, with the black hat."

"Who? George? George Yellowtail is an Apsáalooke Indian. He's on the Fort Landreau tribal council."

"'Lamanite' is our word for Indian," I say.

She shakes her head. "I don't get why you have to make up names for things that already have them."

"It is what I have been taught," I say. "Did it not make you uncomfortable to sit with him?"

Her mouth opens, but it is a moment before she can speak. She says, "Why would . . . ? I mean . . . *wow*. I've known George ever since I can remember. Why would he make me uncomfortable?"

"Because he's a Lamanite?"

We lock eyes, my heart beats twice, and she explodes with laughter. Another heartbeat, and I am laughing too, though I do not know why. It is as if I have been uncorked. For a few moments, I forget where we are. I am back on the ATV, racing along the fence, when the only real things in the world were the two of us and the wind.

She reaches out and touches my knee. It is like an electric shock, running up my thigh and exploding at the base of my spine. I see my own hand lift itself and move toward hers, and cover it. Her hand is alive between my palm and my knee. I can feel her pulse matching my own.

I do not want the moment to end, but after a few seconds, she withdraws her hand and says, suddenly serious, "Jacob, these things you've been taught—that Indians are called Lamanites, and this tree being sacred, and this Zerachiel guy with his ark—do you really believe all of it?"

"I do," I say. But even as I speak, I detect shadowy doubts lurking in the corners of my mind. I push them back. "The Ark will come."

She nods slowly. "I suppose it's no crazier than what other people believe. I mean, Mormons and Muslims and, I guess, some Christian stuff too. That stuff about all those animals fitting into Noah's Ark is pretty wild."

"The Ark was three hundred cubits long."

"How long is a cubit?" she asks.

I show her the distance from the tips of my fingers to my elbow. She thinks for a moment, then says, "Still, there would have to be a lot of animals. I mean, just a pair of elephants would take a lot of cubits, right?" She grins. I don't smile back. Her grin falls away, and she says, "Maybe God used magic to shrink the elephants down to the size of mice."

"The Lord does not use magic."

"I was just kidding."

"You should not kid about such things. And you should not use His name."

"What, 'God'? What do you call him?"

"He is the Lord."

"Huh. And you really think this big boat is going to come and take you away?"

159

"The Day will come, and the Ark will come."

Lynna gives me a long, measuring look. "Jacob, do you think *everybody* else is wrong? Everybody except a few dozen people in Montana?"

"I don't know about everybody else. I just know what I know."

She looks away. "I guess that's all I know, too." For a time neither of us speaks, then Lynna asks, "Is it true what that boy said?" Lynna asks.

I know she is talking about Tobias, but I say, "What boy?"

"Tobias. That he is a prisoner."

"No," I say. "He was in the Pit, and just for a few days."

"What is the *Pit*? Is it really like a dungeon?"

"I don't know what a dungeon is like. The Pit is just a room with a pallet, the Scriptures, and a chamber pot. There is little to do there but pray, which is its purpose."

I hear the creak of iron against iron, the sound of the gate opening. There is no time to hide as Brother Andrew enters the Sacred Heart, pushing his two-wheeled barrow, moving slowly due to his arthritic knees. The barrow is loaded with tools and sacks of bulbs. For a moment, I dare hope that he will not notice us. Brother Andrew can hardly hear, his sense of smell has left him, and his eyes are clouded by cataracts. But my hope is dashed when his milky eyes fix upon us. He peers more closely, frowning as if he has discovered a pair of unfamiliar weeds lurking amongst his tulips.

I clear my throat. "G'bless, Brother," I manage to say.

"Eh? What is that?" His eyes move from me to Lynna, then back to me. "Brother Jacob," he says after a moment.

He sees more clearly than I have given him credit for.

"To be young and callow," he says, shaking his head. "Such wondrous wicked days." With that, he pushes his barrow past us to the flower bed on the far side of the Sacred Heart and busies himself with his planting.

Lynna is staring at him, openmouthed. She looks at me and whispers, "That's the longest beard I've ever seen!"

"Brother Andrew is our eldest," I whisper back. "We should go."

"Are you going to get in trouble?" she asks as we move toward the gate.

"I do not know."

"How old is Brother Andrew?"

"He has ninety-four years."

"Maybe he'll just forget he ever saw us in there."

"His memory is not what it was," I say, even though I know there is no hiding my transgression from the Lord, nor from myself. I have compounded my sins. The Lord struck me down in the woods and forced me to limp and crawl the miles back to the Village, yet still I transgress. Even now as we leave the Sacred Heart, I am imagining when once again the Worldly girl and I can be alone with each other.

22

"We must return to the Hall of Enoch," I tell her.

"Is that all you think about? What you *must* do? Don't you ever get to do what you *want*?"

"You do not understand."

"You got that right," she says. I can tell she is frustrated.

"Do *you* always get to do what you want?" I ask her.

Lynna starts to answer, then hesitates. "I guess not," she says after a moment. "I don't want to get you in trouble."

As we approach the hall, I hear the sound of engines. The tour is returning. One of the Jeeps, with Taylor driving, comes into view and pulls into the parking area, followed by the other vehicles. The visitors get out and mill around.

"You had best rejoin them," I say.

"What about you?"

"I will enter through the rear. We should not speak again."

She gives me a hurt look. "Well, it was nice seeing you."

I watch her walk away. My ankle is hurting. I hadn't thought about it while I was with Lynna, but now the pain has returned. I limp into the back of the hall, hoping I will not be noticed.

"Brother Jacob!" It is Sister Naomi, rather vexed. "Where did you disappear to? We had all those chairs to move!"

"I am sorry, Sister. My leg is causing me pain. I went to rest it for a few moments." The lie rolls off my tongue easily. I wonder when it was that I learned to bear false witness with such facility.

Naomi fixes me with her penetrating glare. For a moment I am convinced that she can read my sins, but she sniffs and turns away. Exaggerating my discomfort, I hobble over to the archway. The tables have been stacked against the walls, and the chairs are arranged in small circles. Father Grace and Congressman Raney are standing at the entrance, greeting the others as they file into the hall. Among them, I see Tobias coming in with his mother. This is the part of the visit where the Worldly folk will be invited to express their concerns, and where we will have a chance to calm those fears.

The visitors are seated in small groups of three or four. Tobias sits with his mother, his sister, and the pink-faced man I presume to be his uncle. Brother Enos crosses the room to join them.

I see Lynna standing with her father. The Lamanite is nearby, talking in a friendly manner with Brother Peter.

"Brother Jacob!" It is Naomi again.

"Sister?"

"If you are well enough to gawk, you are well enough to help me pour tea."

I join her at the serving table and set out a row of cups. Naomi pours, and I arrange the full cups on wooden trays. It takes only a few minutes. Since I am not able to carry the trays into the hall, Naomi dismisses me. I sit on a stool near the archway and stretch out my leg. My ankle is throbbing fiercely.

I try to hear what is being said out in the hall but catch only fragments, as there are too many voices. Father Grace is moving from group to group, laying his hands upon shoulders, listening, speaking in his silken voice. The congressman is also moving through the room, shaking hands and blinding people with his luminous teeth. It is as though they are a team, working together to calm their flocks.

Enos, meanwhile, is listening to Tobias and his uncle, who are taking turns talking. Tobias's mother looks from one to the other, clutching her hands, while his sister stares dully into the air, her hands resting on her swollen belly.

The other groups are led by Brother Caleb, my father, and Brother Peter. I sense that things are going well. Our visitors have been well fed and seem comfortable being here in Nodd. They can see we are not a dangerous cult but rather people of

Faith, who care for the land, and for our children, and who want only peace. I myself am enjoying a sense of pride and good fellowship when suddenly all that is shattered.

"This is bullshit!" Tobias stands up and knocks over his chair.

The hall falls silent for a moment. Everyone is staring at Tobias, who is glaring red faced and slit eyed at his uncle.

"You said I could go with you!"

"Tobias," his uncle says, "I said I would come here and look things over, and I have. I made no promises."

"Bullshit!" Tobias says. His cheeks are burning red.

"Tobias, my business would make it difficult for you to come live with me. I travel most of the year, and you have no friends in Denver. You're safe here. These are good people."

"Bullshit!" Tobias says as if it's the only word he has left.

"Tobias, please," his mother says, holding out her hand.

Tobias slaps her hand away. "Why did you bring me here? I never wanted to come. I hate this place and everybody here. And you—" He turns on his sister. "It's all your slutty fault, getting knocked up. If it weren't for *you*, I'd still be home with my friends instead of in the middle of nowhere with a bunch of crazies."

Tobias's sister looks away from him.

"Please sit, Tobias," says Brother Enos. His voice sounds perfectly calm and reasonable, but I sense something hard and dangerous beneath it.

"Screw you!" Tobias yells, his voice cracking. His eyes

165

roll like those of a trapped animal and land on Congressman Raney. "You have to help me. I'm being held prisoner here. They had me locked in a dungeon! They tortured me!"

Raney stares at Tobias, saying nothing. I cannot tell if he is angry, frightened, or simply embarrassed. Tobias looks over at the sheriff. "You're a cop. They stole my clothes and all my stuff. I want to press charges."

The sheriff appears as nonplussed as the congressman.

"These people are crazy," Tobias says. For a moment he locks eyes with Father Grace, who is standing calmly on the far side of the room, a gentle smile on his face. Tobias points a shaking finger in his direction. "That guy, Father Grace, he's got like four wives, and one of 'em is just a girl. Ask anybody. Ask my mom. Look, you can't leave me here. If you do they'll lock me up again."

One of the congressman's aides is whispering in his ear. Raney brushes him off and says to Sister Judith, "Are you this boy's mother?"

Sister Judith's face looks as if it is about to cave in on itself. She nods miserably.

"Are you here of your own free will?" Raney asks.

"Yes."

"And how old is your son?"

"I'm almost *sixteen!*" Tobias says.

Congressman Raney listens as his aide whispers in his ear again. He nods and says to Tobias, "Son, we did not come here to take children from their home. If you are unhappy, it is a matter you should take up with your mother."

"They locked me in their dungeon!" Tobias says. "That's child abuse!"

Brother Enos says, "Tobias was given a time-out for fighting with one of the other boys."

Raney looks from Enos to Sister Judith, who nods.

Tobias's face grows impossibly redder. "This is *bullshit!*" He kicks his chair and runs out of the hall.

For a few seconds, nobody says anything. Then Tobias's uncle says, "Are you sure you want him to stay?"

Raney approaches Sister Judith. She looks as if she wants to shrivel up and die. He takes her hand and says, "Sister, I know what you're feeling. I raised six kids. Every one of them went through their teens, and every day was a trial. But they all came through okay. I'm sure your son will come around."

Congressman Raney must have made some signal to his companions, for they are all standing, gathering their things. Raney releases Judith's hand and walks over to Father Grace, who has not moved an inch since Tobias's outburst. The two leaders walk out the front door together, followed by the congressman's aides. Enos continues speaking quietly with Tobias's uncle and mother. The other groups slowly return to their conversations. Naomi and the other women are bringing out trays of cups filled with sweet ephedra tea. I look at Lynna. She is staring at Tobias's empty chair, and I wonder what she is thinking.

A few minutes later, one of Congressman Raney's aides comes back into the hall and walks over to Enos and hands him a manila envelope. It looks like the same envelope Enos offered to the congressman earlier. Enos accepts it woodenly. The aide leaves. Seconds later we hear the limousine's tires crackling on gravel as it rolls up the road toward the gate.

Tobias's eruption has cast a pall over the room. Everyone drinks their tea quickly, and soon our visitors are shaking hands and making their way back to their vehicles. I manage to escape through the back without attracting Naomi's attention. I limp around the hall to wait by the front entrance, hoping to exchange a few words with Lynna, but she is already climbing into her father's truck. It is almost a relief. I do not know what I would have said.

I watch the convoy until the last vehicle disappears, then I head back to Menshome. I need to lie down for a while and let my ankle rest. As I pass the Sacred Heart, I see movement out of the corner of my eye. It is Brother Andrew, standing outside the gate, watching me with his milky eyes. Pretending to not notice him, I proceed to Menshome and make my way to my cell.

There is a thick, folded piece of blue fabric on my pallet. I pick it up by one corner and let it unfold. It is a hooded sweatshirt with BRONCOS printed across the front in orange, the same shirt Tobias was wearing when he first arrived. I am perplexed. Tobias's Worldly garb was taken from him the night of his arrival. Who placed this garment here on my pallet, and for what purpose? I notice then a slip of paper on my pillow. I read what is written upon it.

> Hey Jake,
> I just want to say thanks for being nice to me with the cigs and all. This hoodie will look great on you. BTW, that Lynna is not not not! Hasta la vista, baby.
>
> —T.

Clearly the note was written by Tobias. He must have recovered the shirt from wherever his clothing and other Worldly possessions had been hidden. I do not understand why he left it on my pallet. I take the shirt down the hallway to Tobias's cell. He is not there. I look again at the note.

I don't know what "BTW" or "*Hasta la vista*" mean, but it feels like good-bye, and suddenly I am certain that Tobias has left Nodd.

I know I should report this to Enos immediately. But what then? The note would tell Enos more than I care for him to know. I stand undecided in Tobias's cell. What if they catch him and bring him back? I think of Von's dead eyes, and I know I cannot betray Tobias.

I hide the sweatshirt under my mattress, then go to the toilets and tear the note into a hundred tiny pieces and flush them away.

23

Tobias's absence is not noticed until Evensong. Enos directs several of us to search for him within the Village, but he is gone. Brother Peter suggests that he may have stowed away in one of the visitors' vehicles. The search is called off after an hour or so.

"The boy may be with his uncle," Enos says. "But I do not think so. The man showed little interest in taking the boy. If he concealed himself in one of the other vehicles he will be returned to us when he is discovered. If not—" Enos shrugs. "He has done all the damage he is able to do, and one day he will suffer the fate of all apostates."

I want to ask Enos about the manila envelope that he offered to the congressman and was later rejected. But I am certain he will only say it is none of my affair. Later that night, I bring it up with Brother Benedict. He gives me a measuring look and says, "You are observant, as always, Brother. I did not know our offering had been returned. This is not good to hear."

"What was it?" I ask.

"A contribution to the congressman's reelection campaign. I do not know the exact amount, but it was substantial. If it has been refused, it can only mean that we cannot rely on Congressman Raney for protection." He shakes his head. "Father Grace will not be pleased."

I do not sleep for thinking about all that has happened. I rise well before dawn and take myself to the Sacred Heart and kneel at the wall and pray for Tobias, and Lynna, and for forgiveness for my own transgressions. My prayers are swallowed by the darkness. I turn away from the Tree and sit with my back against the low wall and close my eyes and listen to the slow rain of small fruits dropping from its branches.

It is dawn when Brother Andrew awakens me by poking my leg with the handle of his hoe. I mutter an apology and scramble to my feet. I forget my injury for a moment and gasp in pain as I put weight on my ankle. Brother Andrew watches with clouded eyes as I grab my cane from the wall.

"It is Jacob, is it not?" he says.

"It is."

"I saw you with the young lady yesterday, did I not?"

"Yes. She was a visitor. She got lost and wandered into the Heart. I found her here."

Andrew shakes his head. "You need not sully your soul with untruths," he says. I see his yellow-toothed smile through his thin white beard. "I am not one to tell tales." He turns away and shuffles slowly toward the koi pond, while I, grateful and relieved, hobble out of the Sacred Heart.

Tobias does not return to us. Days pass, and then weeks. I think of him often. I imagine him begging on the streets of some godless city. I imagine him dead in a ditch or torn apart by wolves. I remember him standing on the Knob, looking down at the Pison.

One day, while helping Wallace replace some rotting boards on the back wall of the kitchens, I find myself near Sister Judith, and I make bold to ask her if there has been any news of her son. She will not look at me, but she says, "Father Grace has told me to think of other things."

"I pray for him," I say.

She nods, but will say no more.

Two weeks later, Sister Kari, Tobias's sister, gives birth. The child is stillborn.

4

For my loins are filled with a
loathsome disease . . .
— Psalm 38:7

24

Winter descends upon us like a vengeful angel; a blizzard from the plains of Canada buries us in chest-deep drifts of fine, crystalline snow. When the North Road is finally opened, the snow on either side is piled as high as two men.

My ankle has mended. It is still sore, but I no longer need my cane, and I spend two long backbreaking days helping clear the snow from the walkways and the roofs of the Village. On the north side of Menshome is a drift that reaches all the way to the peak of the roof.

Only Brother Andrew, too frail to wield a snow shovel, is thankful for the storm.

"This moisture brings joy to the Tree," he says to me as I shovel snow from around the praying wall. "The bulbs I planted will be spectacular come spring. Father Grace will be pleased."

We are concerned for our flocks. The sheep were moved some weeks earlier to the Low Meadows, and the early blizzard took us by surprise. As soon as the snow stopped, Peter and John trekked to the Meadows on snowshoes. They found the sheep gathered in two flocks separated by half a mile. Each flock had trampled out a circle just large enough to hold them and were huddled together, pawing at the frozen ground to reach the few blades of frozen grass. The larger flock, about three score, was gathered in a low area south of the Spine. The others were farther west, in a basin just north of the high forest. There was no way to get them out through the drifts. Peter and John left the small amount of grain they had been able to carry in their packs.

Peter says we will have to bring them food every day until we are able to get them to the corrals or until the snow melts.

The next night, it sleets. For nearly an hour, we are inundated by an icy downpour. As abruptly as it begins, the sleet is swept away by a frigid wind coming down off the mountains. We awaken to a nightmare fairyland. Every twig of every tree is coated with ice. It is as beautiful as it is deadly.

Almost at once, disaster strikes when Sister Agatha steps out of Womenshome and falls, breaking her arm. Brother Peter spreads what little salt and sand we have on the walkways. I am put to work with a steel bar, chipping ice from around doorways that have been frozen shut.

The frozen rain has formed a hard crust on the snow,

strong enough to support a man. With our snowshoes, Peter, John, and I are able to slide and walk out to the south meadow to check on the sheep. We can hear the first flock bawling unhappily even before they are in sight. As we come up over a low rise, sliding on the hard, slippery crust, I see steam rising from a circular depression about twenty cubits across. The sheep are huddled near one side of the circle, their wool clumped with balls of ice and snow. They appear as a single frozen, steaming, bawling mass, but they have survived. We climb down into the trampled circle. Peter lifts one of the ewes out of the depression to see if she can walk on the crust. She totters only a few steps before her sharp hooves break through the skin of ice, rendering her trapped and helpless. We wrestle the ewe out of the snow and return her to her flock, then leave some oats and hay for them, before going to check on the smaller flock.

The other sheep are harder to get to. The crust in the basin is not strong enough to support us, even with our snowshoes. After a half hour of difficult trudging, we see the circle the sheep have made, but this smaller flock is silent. We quickly find out why.

It is an abattoir, a circle of blood-soaked snow and ice and torn bodies and fluffs of red-stained fleece and ropy entrails. We stand wordlessly, staring with horror at the carnage. The harsh tang of blood smell hangs in the air. I look at Peter; his face is suffused with rage and grief. John looks simply nauseated. I feel much the same.

"Coyotes," John says under his breath.

Peter takes off his snowshoes and climbs down into the ring of gore. He steps carefully through the scattered remains of the flock, examining the trampled snow. John and I remain on the edge. John is fingering the stock of his rifle, staring off at the edge of the high forest, not more than two hundred paces to the south. Peter rejoins us and clamps on his snowshoes.

"Brother Jacob, as I recall, last winter you claimed to have seen a wolf?"

"I *did* see a wolf."

"Have you seen any wolf sign since?"

"The night I injured myself. A wolf paced me for a time."

"And you said nothing?"

"I was delirious. I was not sure it was real. And the first time, when I said what I had seen, I was not believed."

Peter sighs and shakes his head. "You will be believed now. These prints are too big for coyotes."

On the side of the sheep circle facing the forest, he points out a set of bloody paw prints the size of my palm.

"Looks like a loner," Peter says.

"Why would it kill the whole flock?" John wonders aloud.

Peter shakes his head. "It's not normal. Bloodlust, I guess. Wolves usually kill only to eat."

I am thinking, *Not this wolf. This wolf kills to let us know he is here.*

We follow the tracks to where the beast entered the forest.

"It is watching us," says Peter.

I agree with him. I can feel its eyes upon me.

It is a long, quiet walk back. We leave John to guard the larger flock. When we arrive at the Village, Peter recruits several of the Grace to help break a path for the sheep. It takes all day, and the sun has set by the time we herd the last bleating ewe into the corral.

The next morning, John returns with Jerome to the scene of the slaughter. They build blinds and stake out the scene, hoping the wolf will return to feed, but the dead sheep attract only ravens and a pair of young foxes.

25

A cold front moves in that night. It is as if we are being shown the entire range of Montana weather in a matter of days. Temperatures drop below zero degrees for seven nights running. Our hens stop laying, and several of them die from a respiratory disease we have never before encountered. Womenshome's septic tank freezes, forcing the single women to use the facilities in Elderlodge. Jerome and John both suffer frostbite on their ears and fingers from long hours spent in the field hunting the wolf. Although they have brought in three deer for our larders, they have seen no wolf sign, not even so much as a track.

The death of Sister Kari's baby hangs over Nodd as well. The infant was buried in our cemetery without a funeral.

Brother Von chiseled through the frozen loam and dug the grave. It is one of the few tasks with which he is trusted. We are not even told whether it was a boy or a girl. The grave is marked with a simple wooden cross, now buried deep beneath the crusted snow.

On the tenth day of the cold spell, Father Grace gathers us together in the Hall of Enoch to announce that another soul will soon be joining us. Sister Ruth is pregnant.

"It is a miracle," Father Grace says, holding Ruth before him as if displaying a prize. Already the swelling of her womb is visible, and it has been less than three months since she was wed to Father Grace. "The Lord's Quickening," he says. "It is a sign of His forgiveness. Over the past difficult weeks we have been punished for our unspoken sins, for our doubts, for our pride. But now we are forgiven. This child is to be our reward."

Later, I overhear Sister Juliette, Father Grace's second wife, talking to my mother.

"Father may be a prophet, but first he is a man," Juliette says. I can hear anger in her voice. "He had that girl in his bed months ago, even before he left on his mission."

The women move away, and I hear no more of their conversation, but I cannot stop thinking about all the times Ruth looked at me and smiled, even as she was secretly spending her nights in Gracehome. I imagine her face buried in Father Grace's thick beard, and the secret sounds of their fornications. How could I have loved such a girl? The thought sickens me to the core, but at the same time it is liberating. If not for Father Grace, I might have married myself to a girl who would do such a thing.

Still, could I really blame her? Father Grace speaks with the voice of the Lord. Had he asked me to lie with the devil, I might have done so. It is beyond confusing when those who speak for the Lord reveal themselves to be men of flesh.

Fortuitously, with the announcement of Ruth's pregnancy, the weather turns. One day the thermometer reaches forty degrees, and then fifty, and then a glorious day when it is so warm that water runs from the roofs and the last of the ice melts from our trees and the walkways. We lead the remaining sheep, some heavy with lamb, back to the south meadow, where tufts of brown grass are showing once again between the melting drifts. It is not spring, as many weeks of winter lie ahead, but it feels like redemption. I throw myself into my work, as do all the Grace, and I think about Lynna only in the darkest hours of the night.

Our respite from suffering is brief, alas, as a few days later, Sister Mara and Sister Kari steal Father Grace's SUV, leaving behind nothing, not even a note. A week later, the SUV is found abandoned in a suburb of Denver, Colorado.

That Sister Kari ran off was no great surprise. She was despondent over the loss of her child, and she had not been long in Nodd, and she is sister to the apostate Tobias. But Mara had lived here all her seventeen years, and although she was known to be irreverent and bold, no one had ever questioned her devotion and righteousness.

Tobias and Kari's mother, Sister Judith, takes to her bed

and refuses to perform her chores. She is visited by Father Grace, and soon she is back at work in the kitchens. I see her from time to time, trudging expressionlessly from task to task.

As if the apostasy of Sisters Kari and Mara was not enough, a few weeks later, when the temperature has once again dipped into the single digits, Brother Von is apprehended in the milking barn tearing the clothing off the girl-child Sarah, who has fewer than ten summers. Von's heinous act is interrupted by Brother Wallace, who heard the girl's terrified cries coming from the barn. Brother Von is beaten and thrown into the Pit. For days on end we hear his anguished moans and mutterings.

One chilly Greenday morning, as I perform my morning ablutions, I notice that his cries have stopped, and we hear from Brother Von no more.

The absence of Von's cries is almost worse than their presence. No one speaks of it, but we are all affected. Father Grace has cloistered himself in Gracehome. He has not shown himself since he told us of his child to come. Even the younger children seem subdued, their usual laughter and shouting muted and forced.

I thank the Lord for the plentiful work we have to occupy us: feeding and guarding our remaining livestock, cutting and hauling wood for the furnaces, repairing the many leaking roofs, and rebuilding the south barn, which collapsed under the weight of the snow. My ankle is completely healed, and I immerse myself in my labors. I force my thoughts to the task at hand, and work to exhaustion every day, and pray with the intensity of Samson, and sleep the sleep of the dead. The storm, the wolf, the injuries, and the betrayals within our world have consumed us, and I have hardly let my thoughts stray beyond the borders of Nodd.

Enos declares that our edge patrols must resume, and I walk the fence for the first time in months. The snow has receded, but it is still deep in places, and the border is long.

There was a time when walking the fence brought with it feelings of peace. A time when it brought the glory of Heaven into my heart, and soothed my doubts and fears, knowing that this was our land, a holy land blessed by the Lord and protected by Zerachiel, and knowing that the Ark would come for us and take us to a place even greater than that which we have built for ourselves here on earth.

Those days are gone. Now, as I trudge through the snow, I think of Brother Von, and Tobias, and Lynna, and Sister Mara, and the child growing in Ruth's womb, and the dead child born to Sister Kari, and the wolf that may be watching me from the shadows even now. I try to understand how all this has come to be, and I find myself growing angry with the Lord Himself, and this sends sickening waves of guilt coursing through my veins.

When dusk arrives, I have walked only half the fence. I trudge back to the Village through the south meadow, in the dark, avoiding the place where our sheep were slaughtered. I report to Enos in his office.

"You have missed both supper and Babel Hour," Enos says, looking up from a ledger he is studying. His face has a hollowness I have not seen before. This winter has been hard on all. "I feared we would have to go looking for you again."

I do not remind him that the last time I failed to return from my patrol, no one came looking for me at all.

"The snow is still deep in the woods and the low-lying areas," I tell him. "I was able to walk only from the gate to the southwest corner." I tell him of two breaches where trees had fallen on the fence.

"Tomorrow I will send Jerome to make repairs, and you will complete your patrol," Enos says. "Did you see any wolf sign?"

"No. I came upon a deer carcass, but saw only coyote and bobcat tracks."

"Let us hope it has left us," Enos says wearily. "Yvonne is still in the kitchen. Ask her to prepare a plate for you."

I do not go to the kitchen. Instead, I go straight to the Sacred Heart to ask the Lord to calm the storm of thoughts in my head, but kneeling on the icy earth before the Tree is not enough to distract me.

Tired to the bone, I retire without eating.

In the morning, I awaken clearheaded and famished. Brother Will remarks upon my appetite.

"You eat like the wolf," he says.

I have seen how the wolf eats, so I ignore him and finish

my second plate of bread and beans, eating more slowly. I wish there could be eggs, but I have not seen an egg in two months.

Will says, "You are walking again today?"

"So Brother Enos has commanded," I say.

"I would take your place, but for the injury Tobias visited upon me. Samuel says I may never have the full use of my knee." It has been a full season since the day Tobias and Will fought. I suspect he exaggerates his discomfort.

I am not looking forward to this second day of walking. Although my ankle has grown strong, it is sore after yesterday's long trek. I make my preparations slowly and do not leave the Village until an hour after dawn. It is a beautiful day, cloudless and crystal clear, with the temperature promising to rise well above freezing. I decide to begin my walk at the northeast corner, where the walking will be easier. If all goes well, I will reach the Pison by midday, and return by the High Meadow Road. I decide ahead of time not to walk the river. The trail though the Mire would be nearly impassable.

Once again as I plod along, small twinges from my ankle promising to become a throbbing ache, my thoughts go to dark places. I wonder why no one talks about Brother Von. Has he died? I imagine him hollow eyed and gibbering in the catacombs beneath the Tower. Or spirited away to someplace outside of Nodd, confined in a Worldly asylum, sedated by drugs.

By the time I reach the gate, my thoughts have moved from Von to Tobias, and his sister Kari, and Sister Mara, all of whom left Nodd of their own will, apostates doomed to an eternity of torment for their sins.

I pause and look through the gate that leads out of Nodd. The road is an easement that passes through the Rocking K Ranch for half a mile, then curves east to West Fork and the World. The Rocking K cattle have trampled a trail on the other side, while virgin snow heaps up on our side. It would be much easier to walk the fence on the Rocking K side, I realize. I think of the long miles ahead. What difference can it make if I walk on one side of the fence rather than the other? None at all, I decide. I can cross back into Nodd over where the fence meets the Pison.

I unlatch the gate and let myself through. The trail is so well trodden that I do not need my snowshoes; I take them off and strap them to my backpack. Without the snowshoes, walking is much easier. I have gone only a few hundred paces when an ATV track joins the cattle trail. My thoughts turn to Lynna, who now seems like a half-forgotten dream. Was she the one riding the ATV? The tracks are iced over, and there are cattle tracks punching through them, so the ATV must have passed this way a day ago or longer. I wonder if she still thinks of me.

The ATV tracks stay with the fence line. I pass the spot where Lynna and I had our picnic. The repair we made to the fence is invisible beneath the snow, but I know the place from the roll of the land. I shrug off my pack and open it. I have packed biscuits, and a few strips of dried mutton. I sit on my pack with my back to the fence, and chew on dried mutton and gaze off to the north and wonder what Lynna's house looks like. I imagine a sprawling residence filled with modern appliances: computers, radios, televisions, all the things we do not have in Nodd. The things Tobias spoke of with such longing. I hope he has found a life he likes better. It would be sad to burn in Hell for nothing.

The tallowy mutton leaves an unpleasant coating on my tongue. I break a chunk of crust from the snow and chew it. The crunching fills my ears. When I have swallowed the last bits of melting ice, I am struck by how quiet this place is. The light breeze has died away completely, and the only sound left is my breathing. I feel small. I am the only living thing in sight. There is not even a bird in the sky. All around me is whiteness, and the fence at my back. I climb to my feet, don my pack, and continue walking. The sound of my boots on the hard-packed snow and ice drowns out the sound of my breathing.

A few hundred cubits later, the cattle trail and the ATV tracks veer away from the fence and head north. An enormous drift has come up against the fence, reaching nearly to the top. I strap on my snowshoes and leave the cattle trail, making my way around the drift, then returning to the fence. As I near the Pison, the land becomes a series of shallow arroyos filled with snow. In places, the top of the fence disappears beneath the snow. I hesitate to proceed. The river is less than a half mile away, but circumventing the arroyos will require more than a mile of detours. I decide to turn back.

By the time I rejoin the cattle trail, I am thinking that I will be back in the Village in little more than an hour. Enos might question how I could have completed my walk so quickly. I slow my pace, then stop completely as a new thought arrives. I could follow the cattle trail where it curves away from the fence, just far enough to get a look at what Lynna's home looks like. I know it is a foolish idea, and that Enos would not approve, but the more I think about it, the more curious I become. A mile is not so far, and I only want to get close enough to see it.

My body makes the decision for me, and soon I have left the fence behind. The land rises, a gentle slope leading up over a ridge. From the top of the ridge, I look down into a shallow valley. On the far side is a cluster of trees. I see the roof of a barn, and a windmill, and beyond that a series of corrals crowded with cattle. I can see the steam rising off their brown backs.

A thin stream of smoke coils from within the trees, but the house itself is not visible. The cattle trail forks twice as I descend into the valley. I stay with the ATV tracks, and after a few more minutes of walking, the house comes into view.

Lynna's house is very different from our buildings in Nodd. It is long and low, it has many windows, and it is painted an astonishing bright pink. Several vehicles are parked nearby. I can see a small pickup, two ATVs, and a tractor. I imagine myself walking up to the house and knocking on the door. The thought fills me with excitement and fear. I stand watching, hoping to catch a glimpse of Lynna, but there is no movement. After a time, I turn away and trudge back toward the ridge. I am almost to the top when I hear the buzz of an engine. I look back and see a helmeted rider on an ATV bouncing up the trail, coming directly toward me.

26

My first impulse is to run, but I know that I cannot outpace the machine, so I wait, praying that it is Lynna, and not her father or her uncle. As the ATV draws closer, I see strands of blond hair fluttering from beneath the helmet and I know that my prayers have been answered.

Lynna skids to a halt. She pulls off her helmet and shakes her hair free.

"Jacob!" She is smiling. Her cheeks are red; the rest of her face is winter pale. "What are you doing here?"

I feel myself smiling back at her. "Nothing," I say.

She laughs. "You must be doing something! How is your leg? All better?"

"It is healed," I say, though in fact it is rather sore. "How are you?"

"Me? You know, same old, same old. Bored out of my mind. What are you *doing* here?" she asks again.

"I followed the cattle trail," I say, gesturing at the path I am standing upon. "I was just wondering where you lived. Why is your house pink?"

Even though the sky is clear and the sun is shining upon us, a shadow passes across her face.

"That was my mom," she says. "She painted lots of stuff pink after she got her cancer."

"Oh," I say, even though it makes no sense to me.

Lynna laughs at nothing and says, "This is so cool, you coming here! Are you hungry?"

"I should get back," I say, looking over my shoulder toward Nodd.

"Come on, just stay for a few minutes. My dad's in Billings all day, and Cal's off in West Fork for a few hours, so we've got the place to ourselves. I'll make you a quesadilla. Do you like quesadillas?"

"What's a quesadilla?"

"Oh my God, you never had a quesadilla? Do you like Mexican food?"

"I don't know," I say.

"Okay, that's it. You've got to try my quesadillas. They're the best. Get on."

Unable to resist her enthusiasm, I climb onto the machine, backpack and all, and a moment later we are bouncing down the trail toward the pink house.

*   *   *

A quesadilla is two disks of unleavened bread called tortillas, with cheese and other ingredients pressed between them. I sit in the kitchen looking with wonder at all the unfamiliar appliances and decorations as Lynna cooks the quesadilla in a heavy cast-iron frying pan exactly like the ones the women use in Nodd.

"What is that?" I ask, pointing at a white metal box on the counter.

"Bread machine," Lynna says.

"You make bread in a machine?"

"Yeah, you just pour flour and yeast in, and it kneads the dough and bakes it automatically."

I think of the hours the Sisters spend kneading dough by hand. I ask her about another object on the counter.

"That's a food processor for, like, chopping vegetables and stuff. My mom was a great cook. I don't use it much."

"What are all these pink ribbon things?" The ribbons were on display everywhere: refrigerator magnets, a calendar, even a cookie jar with a pink ribbon for a handle.

"That's my dad. He sends money for breast cancer research, and they keep sending us ribbon stuff." She flips the quesadilla. "I hope I didn't make this too spicy. I can't believe you never had a quesadilla."

I hope it is as good as the fried chicken and orange soda we had at our picnic by the fence.

"So what have you been up to all winter?" she asks. "Did that big storm hit you as hard as it did us? We lost thirteen head on the west range."

"Some of our sheep were killed," I say. "By a wolf."

"Really? Cal says he's seen sign, but the cattle we lost just got killed by weather. They got mired in an arroyo over near the river, and we didn't find them in time. They were frozen like Popsicles. My dad was pissed. He had a big fight with Cal over it. Said Cal should've checked that arroyo. It was kind of ugly with the three of us stuck out here. The road was so bad, we couldn't even get to town. I just about went crazy." She slides the quesadilla onto a cutting board, slices it into wedges, and puts the board on the table in front of me. "Let it sit for a minute. The cheese is really hot."

It smells wonderful.

"You want a soda?"

"Yes, thank you."

She takes two cans from the refrigerator and pops open the tops. Coca-Cola. Even in Nodd we have heard of Coca-Cola. I am excited to taste it.

Lynna says, "It gets lonely out here, you know? But I suppose you don't have that problem, what with so many of you."

"I get lonely sometimes. Tobias ran away that same day you came to visit."

"I know. He came here."

I stare at her as a mixture of relief and anger rise up from my belly. I am relieved because a small part of me feared that Tobias had thrown himself from the Knob and been swept away by the Pison. I am angry because the thought of Tobias sitting here in this kitchen with Lynna feels wrong.

"We let him sleep in the bunkhouse. My dad wanted to

drive him straight back to you guys, but then Tobias started telling us stories about how he was treated there—about being locked in the dungeon, or pit, or whatever you call it. My dad made a couple of calls. He talked to Tobias's aunt in Denver, and she said he could stay with her. I guess his sister's there now too. Anyway, the next day we drove him to Billings and put him on a bus. You should try the quesadilla."

I am too shocked by the news of Tobias to reply, so I pick up a slice of quesadilla and take a bite. At first, it is delicious. I chew and swallow, and then I realize that my mouth is burning. I try to speak, but all that comes out is a croak. I grab the Coca-Cola and guzzle half the can. The bubbles from the drink foam in my stomach and I unleash a tremendous belch.

Lynna is laughing so hard tears are coming from her eyes, and the inside of my mouth is burning with the fires of Hell.

27

"I'm sorry," Lynna says as she peels back the top of the que-sadilla slices and picks out the strips of green chili pepper. "I guess you're not used to spicy food."

My mouth is still tingling, and my eyes are watering.

"We eat a lot of Mexican food. Most of our seasonal help is Mexican, you know. I think my mom put peppers in my baby bottle."

"Truly?" I ask.

"Well, not literally, but we eat a lot of jalapeños." She reassembles the quesadilla and says, "Try it now."

Cautiously I take a bite. It's still spicy, but not like before.

"It tastes good," I say. She watches me eat.

"Tobias calls me every now and then," she says. "I guess you never call because you don't have my number," she says.

"We do not use telephones."

"You don't have a phone?"

"No." For some reason this embarrasses me. "Brother Enos has a satellite phone, but it is only for emergencies." I start on a second slice of quesadilla.

"You should get a cell phone," she says, as if I could simply wish it to be so. "Tobias called me a few days ago. He wants me to come and visit. My dad doesn't like him calling. I think he's afraid I'll run off."

Thinking of her running away to be with Tobias angers me.

"Tobias is an apostate," I say, my voice coming out more harshly than I had intended. "He is doomed to burn."

Lynna sits back, startled by my intensity.

"What does that make me?" she says.

"There is hope for you," I say.

She laughs. "Jacob, you are so full of it."

I think she is talking about the quesadilla, and I think about the hellfire that still reverberates on my tongue. I start to reply, to tell her of the Truth that sustains the Grace, and of the Judgment to come, but suddenly I feel foolish and regretful. I know nothing of the World outside of Nodd. When Lynna and the others came to visit Nodd, Father Grace told us that we had to convince them to respect us for our beliefs. Perhaps I need to respect Lynna for hers.

"I'm sorry," I say. "I guess our lives are just different."

"No kidding! Do you ever think about leaving?"

"Leaving what?"

"Nodd."

"Never," I say.

"Because if you ever did, I bet my dad would give you a job."

For the briefest of moments, I imagine it.

"I do not know anything about cattle ranching."

"They're just like big sheep. It's mostly fixing fences."

"In any case, I will not leave Nodd until Zerachiel comes to take me."

Lynna shrugs. "I'm just saying."

She gives me a second can of Coca-Cola, then starts telling me about her friends from school in West Fork. It is hard to listen, because I don't understand a lot of it and it's all about people I will never meet. Lynna sees me drifting off, so she starts talking faster. There is no way I can fit a word in, so I keep eating as she chatters on.

". . . Tara, she's, like, wild. She and a bunch of guys drove all the way to Billings one time just to eat at the Burger Dive, and then on the way back they got pulled over and the cops arrested Jon Harkins because he had a joint on him, but he got let off, and two of the guys on the football team got kicked off because they got caught drinking beer at a Halloween party, and . . ."

By the time I have finished eating, my ears are clogged with names I don't know and my entire body is buzzing. I don't know if it is the Coca-Cola, or the hot peppers, or the conversation. I'm trying to figure out how to make her stop talking when we hear a truck pull up outside. Lynna goes to the window.

"It's Cal," she says.

I think about her knife.

A few seconds later, Cal steps into the kitchen through the side door. He is a small man, I am surprised to see. I am a good two inches taller, although not so thick around the middle. His hair is blond, like Lynna's, but his face is darker and creased from working in the sun, and his eyes are small and hard. When he squints at me his eyes completely disappear.

"Another boyfriend from the freak show?" he says to Lynna. His words sound slurred, and I wonder if he has injured his tongue.

"Jacob just stopped by for a visit," Lynna says. "Jacob, this is my uncle Cal."

"Nice to meet you, sir," I say.

"He's polite, anyway," Cal says. He takes his hat off and slaps it on his thigh to knock the dust off, but there is no dust. It must be a habit. I notice that he is swaying slightly. He notices the cutting board on the table with a few crumbs and bits of cheese on it, and the pepper strips she picked off. "I see Lynna made you one of her tongue-blasters."

"Yes, sir. It was delicious."

Cal smiles in a not-nice way. "Fire and brimstone. Right up your alley." He looks at Lynna. "You gonna make one for your uncle?"

"I'm not your cook, Cal." Lynna is holding herself stiffly, back against the counter, gripping the edge with both hands.

Cal laughs, too loud and too long. He sees my pack and carbine on the floor next to the door.

"You always come armed to visit your neighbors?" he asks.

"There is a wolf," I say.

Cal nods, suddenly serious. "I seen sign. It's them loners you got to watch out for. They get separated from the pack, they'll go after anything. Yellowtail says he took a shot at one over on the Rez last winter. Bet it's the same one—that Indian can't shoot for shit."

I remember that *Yellowtail* is the name of the Lamanite who visited Nodd.

Cal says, "You get a bead on that sumbitch, you shoot straight. Calving season's coming up, and we can't afford to lose no more."

"Yes, sir," I say.

"Speaking of calves, we got some hungry mommas out there. I'd best move some feed. I'll leave you two to get on with your smooching or whatever it was you was about to do." With that, Cal lurches out of the kitchen, and there is an awkward moment of silence.

"He's drunk," Lynna says.

"Is he . . . dangerous?"

"Nah. He does this all the time—goes to West Fork to drink with his buddies, then comes home to act like a jerk.

Anyways, my dad will be home soon. Cal acts nicer when Max is around."

"Do you want me to stay until your dad gets back?"

"It's okay. Cal, he'll just hit his bunk and snore it off." She looks away, and I see she is more embarrassed than afraid. "We have an understanding, me and Cal. He won't bother me. Besides, you have to get back soon, right? You want me to drive you up to the gate?"

I am not comfortable leaving her here with Cal, but she seems to want me to leave, so I nod. A few minutes later, we are back on the ATV, heading up the trail. I look back and see Cal standing outside the corral, watching us.

28

When I return to the Village I feel as if I'm stepping back through time. We have electricity, of course, but mostly it is used only for lighting, driving the well pumps, powering the laundry machines, and running a few power tools. We do not have bread machines or food processors, or televisions or computers. I understand better now why Father Grace does not like us to leave Nodd. An hour or two in the World and already I am tempted.

I go directly to the Sacred Heart to pray. I am surprised by how many others have had the same thought, for the wall is crowded with kneeling figures. I see nine women, including my mother and two of Father Grace's wives. The

Elders Abraham and Seth are there, as are Brother Caleb and Brother Wallace, and a few of the Lower Cherubim. I wonder if something happened while I was gone.

I take a place next to Brother Will, who is kneeling awkwardly on one knee with his bad leg stretched out to the side. He is staring fixedly at the Tree, his lips moving in silent devotions.

The words of the Arbor Prayer come out of me automatically. I have spoken the prayer so many times that my mind wanders as I speak it. I think of riding behind Lynna on the ATV, and I feel my nether parts stirring even as I pray. I squeeze my hands together until they hurt and think of Lynna's hair fluttering in my face. I grind my knees into the hard frozen earth and I think of her smell and I feel the heat of the quesadilla, and I bite my cheek until I can taste blood. It tastes of peppers and cheese.

I think about Cal, of the darkness I sensed within him. I think of the knife Lynna showed me, the knife used for castrating cattle, and I think about our last moments together. As I climbed off the ATV and prepared to walk back through the gate into Nodd, she asked me when I could return.

"I promise not to pepper-blast your mouth again," she said. "Come for breakfast, and I'll make you scrambled eggs with cheese."

The thought of eggs made my mouth water. "Your chickens are laying eggs? Ours haven't been, since the storm. And then they got sick. We have only a few left."

"We buy our eggs at the Albertsons store in West Fork."

"Oh." I was embarrassed not to have thought of that.

Lynna said, "Maybe we could take a couple of the horses out for a ride. Do you ride?"

"I never have," I confessed. I had never so much as touched a horse.

"I'll teach you! When can you come back?"

"I will be walking again in two Landays."

"Tuesday after next, right?"

"Yes."

"That's great! My dad and Cal will both be at the auction in Billings that day."

I told her I would come.

Now, with the Tree watching over me, I squeeze my eyes closed and pray harder, but all I can think of is that I have promised to sin again.

As suppertime nears, the Grace leave the Sacred Heart by ones and twos. Soon only Will and I remain. I nudge him with my elbow.

"What has happened?" I ask.

He looks at me, startled, as if he had not known I was there.

"Why were so many praying here?" I ask.

Will licks his lips and clears his throat. "Father Grace has asked us to offer extra prayers for his son."

"For Von?"

"No, for his new son. Sister Ruth is close upon her time."

"He knows it is to be a son?"

"This is what we pray for." Painfully he climbs to his feet.

"We should wash for supper." He limps off, leaving me alone with the Tree.

Now that everyone is gone, the Tree seems larger and more alive. I feel it can sense my thoughts, as if every tiny branchlet is reaching into my soul. Does the Tree bring my thoughts to the Lord? Or is it a part of the Lord Himself? This has never been clear to me, but now, in the failing light, with the earth beneath my knees drawing the heat from my body, I feel that I am naked before a discrete entity, almost as if the Tree stands apart from the Almighty, and tells Him only what it chooses.

This is absurd, of course, as the Lord is omniscient and omnipotent and there is nothing hidden from His all-seeing eyes. Still, the Tree stands alone, and it has physical form, and I wonder if, like the Tree of Knowledge in the First Garden, it serves more than one master.

Nodd feels different. At supper, the men's voices are slightly muted. Is it weariness after the labors of this long and onerous winter or a reaction to the tragedies that have befallen us? I do not know; I am muted too, not only in my voice but in my soul. Nodd once was a gateway to paradise, the mortal embodiment of the Lord's plan for His children. Now Nodd seems a land sullied by death and lies and rancor. Father Grace has not shown himself in many weeks. No one talks about Von, or of the apostates Mara and Kari, or of Kari's dead child.

Instead, the men mutter of wolves and weather. Two more sheep have been taken, leaving behind only a message written in bloody entrails. Jerome has become obsessed with the wolf. He talks of setting out poison that will kill not only the wolf, but many other creatures as well. He has tried setting out steel traps baited with sheep offal but has caught only a coyote and two raccoons.

"We need a fresh snowfall," he says. "It is impossible to track the beast with all this melt."

I retire early and dream of long blond hairs tickling my face.

The next morning I report to Enos and tell him that all is well along the northern fence line. He listens with little interest. He is looking pale, and I ask after his health.

"I am well, Brother Jacob." He takes a small pouch from a drawer and packs a large pinch of tobacco into the bowl of his briar pipe, then takes his time lighting it from the candle on his desk. He gets a good cloud of smoke going, then says, "I will be glad of spring. This winter has been a trial. How is your ankle?"

"It is well healed. I hardly notice it anymore."

"Praise the Lord." He puffs thoughtfully on his pipe, and I think of Tobias and his cigarettes.

I make bold to ask if he has had any news of the two Sisters who ran off.

"They are back in the World, no doubt, whoring and sinning their black hearts out. Sister Judith is well rid of her wicked offspring, as are all the Grace. As for Sister Mara—"

He shrugs. "Father Grace did his best to bring her to the Lord. Even he is capable of failure."

As he failed his son Von, I think. I would ask him what has happened to Von, but I am afraid of what I might hear.

Enos sees something in my face.

"And what of you, Brother? Does your faith burn brightly?"

"Always," I say, because to say otherwise would be unthinkable.

Enos snorts smoke. "It would not be unusual for one of your age to experience doubts, as did your friend Tobias."

"He was not my friend," I say.

"You know that you can always share your thoughts with me."

"I thank you," I say, even as I am thinking that Enos is the last person in Nodd to whom I would confess.

"You wonder as to Brother Von," he says, and I feel as if he has ripped the thought directly from my head. Enos smiles through a cloud of smoke. "Why should you not? I will tell you, but I will ask you not to speak of him to others."

I manage to nod, keeping my face carefully still.

"Zerachiel has taken Brother Von's soul."

He looks intently at me, searching for my reaction. I am like a stone.

"Von hanged himself in the Praying Pit with a noose made from strips of his own clothing. Father Grace buried him next to Sister Salah in the courtyard behind Gracehome."

Enos leans back in his chair. "As this has been such a difficult time, Father Grace felt that the news of Von's suicide would cause the Grace unnecessary anguish."

"Not knowing is worse," I say.

"That may be," he says, "but the decision is made." He draws on his pipe, then frowns at the bowl. "And so we go on, as if Von were never born. When Father Grace's new son arrives, we begin anew. Do you understand?"

"I . . . I think so," I say. "Von's soul was lost, but now it will be reborn?"

"Father Grace has long foretold that he will have a son who will join him on the Ark. The time of Zerachiel's coming is nigh. These past few months have been the Lord's final test of the Grace. We must stand strong; we must stand together." He takes a final puff from his pipe, scowls, and taps the ashes out onto his desk.

"This year's tobacco crop is acrid. I must speak to Brother Peter."

"There may not be a next year," I point out.

Enos smiles sourly. "One can only pray."

29

The next twelve days pass by ponderously, each one almost indistinguishable from the next. The snow cover continues its slow recession; the Meadows become a maze of melting drifts snaking through brown grasses. Because of the wolf attacks, the sheep must be guarded night and day. Every morning, Jerome and I and other Cherubim herd the sheep a mile or more to where they can forage, then guide them back to their corrals before dark. We do our work, we are strong, we labor together. An invasion of field mice decimates our stores of wheat, and the women spend long hours sorting mouse droppings from what will become tomorrow's bread. We eat the last of our apples and squashes. Although there is no danger of running out of food, our meals become less varied as our stores are depleted. We have a surfeit of beans and mutton. Father Grace remains cloistered with his family, awaiting the blessed event. We are all waiting, as welcoming a new child into our midst will be the first joyful event in many months.

Landay arrives in a haze of ice. It was warm last night, the temperatures rising higher than they had been since October, but a chill descended in the early hours of the morning, and the air dances with ice crystals. It is eerily beautiful as I head out of the Village. The bushes, the trees, and the walls of the buildings all look as if they have been sprayed with sugar frosting. My boots are loud on the ground, every step crackles, and the half-frozen droplets suspended in the air soon leave a wet sheen on my face and dampen the surface of my garments. I head straight up the North Road.

The moment I step through the gate I feel a space form within my breast, as if a door has opened and my heart has room to beat freely. I follow the fence, feet crunching on the icy, cattle-trodden earth, shedding the concerns of Nodd with each step. Father Grace falls away, as do Ruth, and the wolf, and the sheep, and Enos, and Von, and the sadness. Out here, life is simple and clean. There is only the land, the walking, and Lynna. By the time I reach the place where the cattle trail veers from the fence, the icy fog has dissipated. The sun cuts through the haze, and I hear the hopeful whistle of a marmot seeking signs of spring.

I follow the cattle trail up the long, low rise. The valley comes into view. Trees and the tops of buildings jut up through a lake of mist, as the fog has yet to leave the lowlands. I stand at the high point for a time, imagining Lynna in her house. What is she doing? What is she wearing? What is she thinking? It is a great mystery; I know so little of the life she leads.

A gust of uncertainty strikes me, and there is a moment when I almost turn back. I could walk the fence, as is my duty, and return to the Village, to the fold, to the Grace, whose love for me is as indisputable as the land itself. I think of my mother, and all the people with whom I have spent my life. I think of the Tree, waiting for me to spill my sins onto its branches. I think of the firm mattress upon which I have dreamed, and that delicious weariness that comes after a hard day in the fields.

I think of my father. What would he say, were he to see me now? Would he be surprised, or are my sins no more than what he expects from me? I feel a node of resentment heating my belly, and I crush it. I do not want to sully this day with such broodings. If I am to sin, then I might as well sin avidly, hungrily, ardently.

Lynna opens the door, and she looks wrong. For a moment I think she is a different person, and I step back. She smiles and laughs then, and I know it is her, despite the smooth face, the pink lips, and the dark lines framing her blue eyes.

"Come on in," she says, stepping aside to make room. I

enter the house. It is warm, and the air smells of baking. I take off my pack. I am trying to understand what has happened to her face. Her hair is pulled back and tied with a piece of fabric. She is wearing tight blue jeans and a fawn-colored shirt with many white buttons.

Because I don't know what else to say, I ask her why her face looks so odd.

"Odd?" she says. "You don't like it?"

"I did not say that. I am startled, is all."

"Well, I put on some lipstick and stuff. You know, to impress you with my ravishing beauty."

"I am always impressed with your beauty," I say, and from her expression I know that for once I have said exactly the right thing.

"You are very sweet, Jacob," she says.

"The Grace do not wear paint. I am not used to it."

"Paint? That's what you call makeup?"

"It looks very nice," I say, although I prefer her without it.

"Ha! Liar!"

I understand that she is joking, so I laugh.

"Are you hungry?"

I remember that she promised to cook some eggs, so I nod.

"Guys are always hungry," she says. "Tobias ate like a horse the day he was here. I made pancakes for him the morning he left. He scarfed down a dozen of them."

I experience an unpleasant twinge as I picture her cooking for Tobias.

"Have you heard from him?" I ask.

"No. Actually, I'm kind of worried. He used to call once or twice a week, but it's been, like, three weeks. I tried to call him, but his cell is disconnected. I hope he's okay."

I say nothing.

"So . . . scrambled eggs? My famous scramble?"

"That sounds good," I say, wondering how many eggs I will have to eat to impress her.

I have never seen anything quite like the concoction Lynna assembles. She cracks eggs into a large bowl. Eight eggs as bright and white as snow. Our eggs in Nodd, when the hens are laying, are brown. She adds handfuls of crumbly white cheese, chunks of smoked ham, chopped onion and green pepper, and a cup of diced cooked potato.

"I usually put some jalapeños in, but I promised not to burn you."

"Thank you," I say.

She melts an enormous cube of bright-yellow butter in a large frying pan. When the butter is sizzling, she pours in the whole bowlful of eggs and other ingredients into the pan, covers it, and turns down the heat.

"It's got to cook for a bit," she says.

My mouth is watering.

Lynna opens the top of the bread machine and the smell of baking instantly becomes stronger. She lifts out an oddly shaped loaf of bread and sets it on a cutting board.

"See?" she says. "I put flour, water, and yeast in the machine before I went to bed last night, and here it is. Pretty cool, huh?"

I nod, impressed. She gives the eggs a stir, then cuts the bread into six thick slabs. Inside, the bread is almost blinding in its whiteness. I am eager to taste it, but I think I should wait for the eggs. As I sit there swallowing saliva, Lynna puts out a dish of butter and a glass jar containing what looks like clear reddish jelly.

"Homemade jelly," she says. "My mom's recipe, but I made it myself."

"We make everything ourselves in Nodd," I tell her.

"Yeah, I kind of got that feeling when I was there. You guys must be really healthy."

"We have had our share of illness," I say, thinking of Brother Abraham's monthlong chest cold.

"So what do you do if you get sick?"

"We have a healer, Brother Samuel, who mends wounds and offers palliatives to the ailing."

"What if something really serious happens, like a heart attack? Or cancer?"

"I do not know," I say. "We have had no deaths from disease since Father Grace's son Adam died, and that was before my time. Sister Salah took her own life. We have lost two infants in childbirth. No one dies until the Lord chooses to take them into His arms."

Lynna stares at me wordlessly for a moment, then gets up to stir the eggs again.

"Must be nice," she says.

"What do you mean?"

"To just figure that whatever happens is what God wants. I know when my mom got cancer, she really didn't want to die. She did everything she could to stay alive—radiation, chemo, praying, the whole deal. It didn't work, and she felt really bad, like she'd failed. So it must be nice to think there's nothing you can do about it anyway."

"I have never thought of it that way," I say.

"But my aunt, she got appendicitis and got really sick before she went to the doctor. They told her if she'd waited another day, she would have been dead, but they operated on her and now she's fine."

"The Lord must have intended for her to go to the doctor."

"I suppose. But if you got appendicitis in Nodd, what then?"

"Brother Samuel would care for me."

"What, give you a cup of tea and pray?" She snorts. "I don't think that would help."

"The Grace are different," I say. "Maybe we don't get appendicitis."

"Lucky you." Neither of us speaks for a few seconds. Lynna takes the eggs off the stove. She scoops half of them onto a plate and sets it before me, then makes a plate for herself, with only half of the remaining eggs. "There's more if you want," she says as she sits down across from me.

Something has gone out of the room, and I am not sure what it is, but I still have my appetite. The eggs are delicious.

I try to eat slowly, because I do not want her to think I eat like Tobias. The bread is warm, and softer than any bread I have eaten before.

"Try the jelly," she says.

I spread a spoonful of jelly on my bread. It is as sweet as honey, yet tart at the same time, with a fruity scent that reminds me of apples.

"This is very good," I say.

She shakes some red liquid from a small bottle onto her eggs.

"What is that?"

"Hot sauce. You wouldn't like it."

I try a few drops anyway. She is right. I gulp my water.

We eat without talking for a minute or two. I feel bad that I might have said something to offend her, but then I look up and she is smiling at me again. I smile back.

"You are a very good cook," I say. "These are the best eggs I have ever eaten."

That makes her smile even more. The pink lipstick has mostly worn off of her lips, and she looks more like the Lynna I know. She sees that my plate is almost empty and scoops the rest of the eggs onto it. I eat them, and another slice of bread with jelly as well.

As she piles the dishes in the sink, she asks, "Still up for a ride?"

For a moment, I think she is referring to the ATV, then I remember we talked about riding horses. We have no horses in Nodd. Brother Peter says they eat more than they are worth.

"You would have to teach me." I am nervous. I do not want to look clumsy or foolish in front of Lynna.

"You can ride Chico's nag. She's gentle as a lamb. Here." She grabs an apple from a bowl on the counter and tosses it to me. I am astonished by how red and shiny and perfect it is. Our apple trees in Nodd produce only oddly shaped, mottled fruits, more yellow and green than red, and by midwinter they are always wrinkled and going bad. "Put it in your pocket. It'll help you get to know Lily." Seeing my confusion, she adds, "Lily's the horse."

30

"She's really gentle," Lynna says. "Give her some apple. She'll love you."

I twist the apple to snap it in half as Lynna lifts the saddle onto the horse. Lily is enormous. Not as massive as our brace of oxen, but taller. Her coat is mostly white, with pale brown blotches scattered over her hindquarters, and gray hairs around her snout. Lynna makes adjustments to the strap holding the saddle to the horse's back. She is wearing dark-brown leather gloves that fit her hands so precisely, it is as if they are a second skin. My homemade deerskin gloves look crude by comparison.

I take them off and offer Lily half of the apple. Lily takes it from my palm delicately, her bristly lips brushing my palm.

"Pet her on the neck," Lynna says. "She likes that."

I stroke the horse's neck, feeling her coarse hair and the powerful muscles beneath it.

"Just get to know her for a minute while I saddle up Edgar." Lynna moves down two stalls and starts talking to another horse. I feed Lily the other half of the apple.

"My name is Jacob," I tell her in a soft voice. Lily snuffles and shifts her feet. I can feel the heat coming off her. There are horses in the Bible. Joseph had horses, and the Pharaoh's men, and Zerachiel's own chariot will be drawn by flying horses of silver and gold. I run my hand along Lily's shoulder and imagine her sprouting wings. Does she know I am about to climb onto her back?

Lynna leads Edgar out of his stall, and we walk the horses out of the barn into the sunlight. The fog is gone, and the air is as bright and sharp as crystal. It is warmer, too. I take my hat off and stuff it in my pocket. Lynna shows me how to place my foot in the stirrup. Clumsily I bring my right leg up over the horse's back and seat myself on the saddle. Lily snorts her displeasure at my awkwardness. I grip the knob on the saddle and sway from side to side as she shifts her feet nervously.

Lynna swings easily and gracefully onto Edgar. She shows me how to hold the reins.

"We'll take the cattle track through the woods. You don't have to do anything—I'll go first, and Lily will follow." She makes a kissing sound and gives the reins a shake. Edgar moves off along the corral fence. Lily falls in behind him. The feeling of riding atop a giant animal both terrifies me and makes me feel powerful, as if the strength of the animal is rising up through my bones. I hold the reins slack. As promised, Lily needs no guidance; she simply follows Edgar.

The snowy ground looks very far down, but with every step, my fear of being thrown to the earth eases. Soon I am thinking less of the beast beneath me and more of the wonder that surrounds me. Mostly my eyes are fixed upon Lynna, who sits so lightly in her saddle that it seems she will float away.

We follow the trail along the wooded north face of the valley, through tall, close-growing ponderosas and cedars. There is little snow on the ground here. It is so densely wooded that most of the snow was caught by the trees and is now melted.

"My dad's been talking about logging the north slope," Lynna says over her shoulder. "I told him if he tried it, I'd chain myself to a tree."

"Would you really?"

"Damn right I would."

I shudder to hear her speak so, but I say, "We log our forests. It is the only way to get wood."

"My dad wants to do it for the money. He worries about money all the time."

"My father once worried about money. He was a lawyer, and money weighed heavy on his soul. It was not until he gave it all away and we came here to Nodd that he found peace."

"He gave away *everything*?"

"Everything save for my mother and me."

"Expensive peace," Lynna says. "But so long as he's happy, I guess that's cool."

I think of my father's stern, disapproving features and try to recall the last time I saw him filled with joy.

The trail enters a small oblong clearing. We are surrounded by trees of extraordinary stature, even taller than the tallest trees of Nodd. It feels like a grand temple, a footprint of the Lord. Above us is an oval of brilliant blue sky. Lynna pulls up, then slaps her thigh and makes a hand gesture. Lily moves forward to stand close on her left side. Our knees brush against each other.

"I like this place," Lynna says, her voice almost a whisper.

It is not necessary for me to reply. We sit in our saddles without speaking, the only sounds the breathing of the horses and the faint hiss of a breeze tickling the tops of the pines.

"In the summer it's filled with ferns and flowers," she says. "I come here to think."

"What do you think about?"

She doesn't answer for several seconds. I hear a squirrel chatter. Lily paws at the snow and lowers her head to sniff at the disturbed pine duff.

I feel Lynna brush my sleeve, then grasp my hand in hers, her fine riding glove wrapping my crudely sewn deerskin.

She says, "I think about nothing."

I know what she means. I have spent many hours kneeling before the Tree, thinking of nothing as my mouth speaks the words of the Arbor Prayer. The repetitive movements of my lips free me to have no thoughts, to embrace the peace that comes with that blankness of the mind.

"Do you feel the presence of the Lord?" I ask.

"I feel the presence of something," she says. "But I think it's more like when I'm here, I know that my life is only a small part of something huge. I don't know if it's God or what." She looks at me. "What do you feel?"

"I feel your hand," I say, surprising myself.

She gives my fingers a squeeze, holds my hand for a moment, then lets go. "This is the first time I've ever brought anybody here."

"You did not come here with Tobias?"

She smiles and shakes her head. "Tobias was only here for a day. Besides, he isn't my type."

"What type is that?"

Lynna laughs. "I like those dark, broody cult boys." She gives her reins a twitch. Edgar continues through the clearing; Lily follows. The trail winds through the tall trees, around a jagged outcropping of shale, then makes a right turn and descends sharply into a draw. Lily, sure-footed and steady, follows Edgar into the draw, where the snow is almost up to her belly, then up the other side onto a ridge. Lynna stops and looks back.

"How are you doing?"

"Good," I say, although I am somewhat sore from the saddle, and from using muscles I have never used before.

"This ridge leads up to the north pasture. We'll be back in ten minutes or so. Can you handle it?"

I nod. I will be glad to get my feet back on the ground.

We start moving again, but have gone only a short distance when Lily snorts, wheels abruptly, and leaves the trail.

I grip the horn of the saddle as her forelegs plunge into the deeper snow. Her hind end comes up. I lose my grip and fall forward onto her neck. I hear Lynna shout as I slide over Lily's head and tumble through the air. I land on my face and feel something strike my forehead.

Dazed, I rise to my feet, floundering in hip-deep snow, trying to understand what has happened. Lily has made it back to the trail and is running back the way we came while Lynna is frantically trying to control Edgar, who is jerking at his bridle, looking around wildly. It lasts only a couple of seconds. She gets him back under control, but he is making huffing sounds and his eyes are rolling. Holding the reins tightly with one hand, she strokes his neck and speaks to him in a low, soothing voice. I slog through the snow and climb back onto the trail.

"Are you okay?" she asks me.

"I think so."

"You're bleeding."

I put my hand to my forehead, then look at my glove. It is dark and wet with blood. Lynna swings off her horse, still holding the reins, and walks over to me.

"Let me have a look." She examines my forehead with a concerned expression. "It looks like a shallow cut. You must've hit something when you fell." She wipes away the blood with the ball of her thumb. "A branch, or some ice. Here." She digs in one of her vest pockets and comes out with a tissue. "Hold this against it. Are you dizzy or anything?"

"No. What happened?"

"Something spooked Lily. She can be a real scaredy-cat."
She looks into the woods to the left of the trail. "Probably just
a squirrel. Stupid horse. I'm really sorry."

"It was not just Lily. Your horse is nervous, too." I cross
the trail and wade through the snow into the trees. I have
gone only about ten paces when I smell blood.

I find the deer carcass another ten paces farther in. Most
of the animal has been eaten. The area around it is trampled
with bloody, palm-size paw prints. I touch the remains of the
deer; it is soft, unfrozen. A recent kill. I look back through the
trees at Lynna, who is watching me from her horse.

"Wolf," I say.

We ride back double, my chest and hips pressed against
Lynna's back.

"What about Lily?" I ask.

"She'll find her way home."

A gust of wind whips her hair across my face. I catch a
strand between my lips, hold it for an instant, then let go.
"Unless she runs into the wolf," I say.

"I doubt a wolf would go after something as big as a horse.
At least, that's what my dad says. He says they prey on smaller
animals, or sick animals that are easy to catch."

"I hope he is right."

"That's why we're worried, come calving season. A wolf
would take down a calf easy."

"They kill sheep, that's for sure. Have you ever had
wolves here before?"

"No. There are a couple of big packs in Yellowstone, but that's more than two hundred miles from here. Cal says this wolf is probably a young male who got driven out of his pack, then wandered up this way. He's pretty sure there's just the one."

"He must be lonely," I say.

Back at the house, Lynna cleans the cut on my forehead, saying, "It's not deep, but you're going to have a bruise for a while." She covers it with a bandage. Her face is only inches from mine. I notice the small furrow between her eyebrows, what I once heard my mother call the *crease of caring.*

I raise my hand to her brow and smooth it with my thumb. She is startled, but she does not move.

"Pressing out my worry line?" she says. That must be another name for it: *worry line.*

"Do you worry a lot?" I ask.

"I worry about you."

"Me? Why?"

"Because you live in Nodd. Because you don't know anything about the world. Because you fall off of horses."

"I fell off *one* horse. Once."

"You've only *ridden* once." She grins, and happy lines crinkle the corners of her blue eyes. "That means you fall off every time you ride."

I kiss her on the lips.

I *kiss* her.

31

Our lips are one and I am consumed. I fall like Sister Salah dropping from the Knob, but there is no bottom, no river, no rock. I fall and I fall, and I never want it to stop. In the distance I can hear the beating of my heart, and I can smell the smell of her hair, and the soft, silent click of our teeth touching echoes through my bones, and then it is over, and we are looking at each other, breathing each other's warm breath, and still I am falling.

"Wow," she says. "I didn't think you were gonna do that." She laughs. "Your beard tickles."

"I'm sorry," I say, although I am not sorry at all. I want to do it again, and I do. This time, she kisses me back hard, our lips grinding together, and nothing else is real. There is a sound growing in my head, water tumbling over boulders. I do not know if I am standing, sitting, or still falling. My arms grasp her and pull her against me as if we can become a single entity. My hands run down her back and grasp her hips and pull her hard against me, pressing my swollen phallus against her—

And suddenly her hands are on my chest, pushing hard, and we are apart, gasping.

"Whoa," she says. "Easy!"

Breathing heavily, my mouth open and wet, I stare back at her dumbly.

"That was intense," she says, forcing a little laugh.

I don't know what to do.

"It's okay," she says, pushing back a strand of hair and straightening her shirt.

A prickling in my belly grows and becomes embarrassment as I realize what has happened. The lustful beast inside me has shown itself. My groin has become an inflamed and painful knot; my cheeks are burning with shame and desire. I wipe my mouth with my sleeve and look away.

"Jacob, it's okay," she says again. But it is not okay.

"I should go," I mumble. My tongue feels different, as if it belongs to someone else. Some animal.

"Okay, but you have to promise to come back. Okay?"

I do not trust myself to respond.

"I'll drive you up to the fence, okay?"

The beast within me is thinking of being pressed against her body one more time. Slowly, carefully, I put on my jacket and pick up my pack and my rifle. I feel like a great clumsy animal, as if my every move threatens to destroy all that I touch.

"I can walk," I say.

"Are you sure?"

"Yes." I open the door and step outside. I am surprised to find the sun high in the sky. It feels as if it should be night. Lynna follows me out, her crease of caring deep on her brow.

"It was really nice seeing you, Jacob."

Nice? How can it be nice?

"I'm sorry," I say, staring at the ground.

"You don't have to be sorry. I liked kissing you. Seriously."

How could she have liked it? Is she as base as I?

"I want to show you something before you go. Over here."

I follow her around the side of the house.

"See?" she says, pointing at a tree growing near a fence.

I look at the tree, not understanding. It is a small tree, no more than twice my own height, bare of leaves, its many branches dotted with small shriveled fruits. And then I see it. It is a miniature version of the Tree.

"It's a crabapple, like the one you showed me, only not so humongous." She picks a fruit and holds it out in the palm of her hand. "Crabapples. These are what I made the jelly out of."

The knuckle-size fruit looks exactly like the fruits of the Tree. I look from the fruit to the small tree, struggling to understand.

"*Our* Tree is *the* Tree," I hear myself say.

"Yeah, and it's *huge*. I mean, I don't think I've ever seen a crab tree that big, ever. You must fertilize the heck out of it."

"This is not the Tree," I say.

"I know. My dad planted this the day I was born. But I was thinking—you know your tree? I think my grandfather planted it."

"What?" I am confused.

"Yeah, you guys—I mean, Father Grace—bought your land from my dad. It used to be part of our ranch. Then when my grandfather died, my dad needed money for taxes, so he sold off the south ten sections. You know where your village is now? That's where my grandparents' house used to be. It's gone now of course, but I think that tree is the same one that used to be in their front yard. My grandfather planted it when my dad was born, and that's how come my dad planted this one when *I* was . . ." She trails off, seeing something in my face. "Jacob?"

She is smiling, but the crease between her eyebrows is deep as a cut. I feel I am seeing her clearly for the first time, and I am horrified by how close I have come to the abyss. The heat I feel in my loins is the fire of Hell. I have allowed myself to tempted, to be seduced by this Worldly woman. As Adam allowed Eve to tempt him to betray their Lord, so have I been drawn into lechery, grunting and panting like a ram in heat. Was this what happened to Von? Am I *becoming* Von?

"This is a false tree," I say. My voice sounds like gravel sliding off a shovel. "And you are false as well. I should not have come here. You think me a fool, and you are right."

Her face crumples, and I know I have hurt her but I do not care. I turn my back and walk away from her, toward Nodd. As I trudge up the long, sloping cattle trail, my mind stutters and whirls with the shameful things I have done, from my foolish, lustful thoughts of Ruth, to the first time I ventured forth from Nodd to eat Worldly fried chicken, to the hellfire of the quesadilla, to the unspeakable transgressions of today. What will I have to do to seek forgiveness? I imagine the sweet sting of cedar needles raking my back, and I know it will not be enough. I imagine myself confessing my sins to Brother Enos, and I quiver with fear at what he might do. Will Brother Samuel make scars beneath my brow and tear away my soul, as he did to Von? Or will I be cast into the Pit to howl and gnash my teeth until the pain of my transgressions becomes too much to bear and I hang myself with strips of cloth from my sullied trousers? Better to throw myself from the Knob, to shatter my skull on the tumbled boulders of the Pison, or lie naked in the forest and let the wolf lap tainted blood from my yawning carcass.

I hear the sound of the ATV, growing louder. Seconds later, Lynna pulls up alongside me. I keep walking. She pulls ahead and stops, blocking my path.

"Jacob, I'm sorry," she says.

"I do not wish to talk to you," I say.

She climbs off the machine. "I'm sorry if I offended you about your tree," she says. "I'm sorry I made fun of your religion."

"I should not have come here."

"Why?"

The plaintive note in her voice weakens my resolve, but I say, "Because you are doomed, and you would doom me as well."

She draws back as if I have slapped her. I feel a twinge of regret. I push it away and move to walk around her.

"Jacob, tell me what I can do to make things right. Please!"

That stops me.

"You would have to accept the Lord with all your heart and soul, beg His forgiveness, renounce the ways of the World, and come to Nodd on bended knees and request sanctuary."

"And then what?"

"The Grace offer sanctuary to those who are willing to do these things. You would become one of us, and live a righteous life, and await the coming of Zerachiel."

"Are you saying the only way we can be friends is if I join your . . . group?"

"If you do not, you will be destroyed."

Lynna bites her lip and shakes her head slowly. I see tears in her eyes.

"Oh, Jacob, can you even hear yourself?"

"Yes," I say. I walk around her and continue toward Nodd. Behind me, I hear her start the ATV. The whine of its engine is loud at first, then fading, and soon I hear only the crunch of my boots on the packed snow.

32

A copse of stunted cedars grows in a shallow draw not far
from the Village. I cut several branches and spread them on
the snow. I take off my jacket and my two shirts. The skin
of my bare torso puckers from the cold. I lay myself upon
the prickly boughs and stare up into the deepening blue sky.
I imagine Zerachiel descending on his golden chariot, seeing
me spread-eagled in my icy bower, passing over me, reject-
ing my sullied soul. I know that to gain passage on the Ark,
I must cleanse myself, make myself clean. I think of Father
Grace in the desert, in the hailstorm. I think of his four days
and three nights of agony, and how he entered his ordeal as
the worst of sinners and emerged as a prophet. I tear the bandage from my forehead and scratch at my wound until I feel

warm blood running down my temple. I watch the blue sky darken as my naked breast grows cold and the sharp needles of the cedar boughs work their way into my back and the flow of blood from my brow ceases. For a time my body shivers violently, then that stops as well.

I open my eyes. There are stars, painfully intense, and all around me darkness, and I know I have been sleeping. The night sounds are crisp and bright: wind scraping the tops of the cedars, my breath rasping past my lips, and the distant hoot of an owl, sharp as a blade. I wonder if my body is frozen. I will my right hand to move. My fingers curl without shattering, but they feel distant, as if my arm is miles long. I am still alive. A part of me is disappointed.

I detect a glimmer of moonlight through the branches. From its height above the horizon, I guess that most of the Grace will be at supper.

Do any of them search for me? Am I missed?

A part of me does not care. I imagine them finding my scavenged corpse come spring, and the thought brings with it a glimmer of satisfaction. As for my soul . . . am I as lost as Lynna? If so, then it matters not when I die.

I hear a new sound, the whisper of padded feet on the snow. I turn my head to my right. At first I see nothing but the dark shapes of the trees, then a glint of moonlight reflected from an eye. Not ten cubits from where I lie half naked on my frozen bed of cedar boughs stands the wolf, watching me. Our eyes meet.

I once thought the wolf to be an invader, an evil presence come to plague us, but now I wonder if he is one of Zerachiel's messengers, come to cleanse the Grace of a sinner.

I am not afraid. If the beast chooses to take me now, then so be it. The wolf knows I see him, but he does not move. We both wait; for what, I do not know.

After a time, my eyes lose the shape of the beast in the shadows, and I wonder if he is really there. Then I see some slight movement, a sway of his shoulders, or the flick of a tongue, and his form once again materializes. It is during one of these periods of clarity that I see his ears prick up. His head turns. I can see his long snout in profile. He takes one last look at me and melts away. His absence leaves a vacuum within the grove, and I am cold again, and the shivering resumes. Moments later, I hear the voices of men. The beam of a lamp scatters through the branches. I hear boots crunching through the crust, and the light strikes my eyes, and behind it I see my father's face.

How long did the wolf and I remain together in that cedar grove? In my memory, it was hours, but it could not have been so long, because Evensong has only just ended when my father carries me into Elderlodge, where I am wrapped in layers of heated blankets and forced to drink quantities of hot honeyed tea. My mind is working sluggishly, and I am able only to nod and shake my head to their questions. Brother Samuel is there. My mother brought the tea. Others are nearby, talking. I understand only fragments of what I hear.

". . . hypothermia and frostbite . . ."

". . . a miracle he is alive . . ."

". . . thank the Lord we came across his tracks . . ."

Brother Samuel is bending over me, examining my forehead. Someone is massaging my feet. I think it is my father. I cannot remember the last time my father touched my flesh.

". . . the Lord's will . . ."

". . . delirious. He had taken off his garments and made himself a bed . . ."

I feel something stab into my forehead and I think of Von. I struggle, but the blankets are too heavy, too tightly wrapped. I see a needle in Samuel's hand. I do not care if I die, but to have my soul taken while my body yet lives is terrifying. I curse and snap at him, and he strikes me, a slap to my cheek, and someone grasps my head from behind to hold it steady.

"Jacob!" My mother's voice cuts through the fog of fear. "Hold still and let Brother Samuel stitch your wound."

Is that what she thinks he is doing? I manage to gasp out a few words: "He lies. He lies. He—"

A moist cloth smelling harshly of chemicals is clapped over my mouth, and the abyss opens, and I am swallowed.

5

And he walked in all the sins of his father, which he had done before him.

—1 Kings 15:3

33

I am dead inside.

It was not Brother Samuel who killed my soul. He only stitched the cut on my forehead. I am dead inside because I have killed myself. I move from task to task, working, praying, eating, and trying to sleep. When sleep comes, hours after I lay my body to rest, it is a sleep of nightmares and terrors. When I eat, the food is tasteless. I may as well be eating leather and dirt. When I pray, my mouth moves, but my heart is lost in a quagmire of mortification and unspeakable longing.

Brother Enos questioned me at length. *Why did the searchers find your footprints leading from the gate to the cedar grove? What were you doing outside the fence?* I told him I remembered nothing, neither how I injured my head nor where I was when it happened. He looked at me long and hard, but I told him no more.

I do remember, of course. Would that I could forget! But there is no question of confessing my sins. I am beyond that, my shame too deep, my sins too vast.

Father Grace has taught us that no sin is unforgivable if we are truly repentant, and therein lies the rub. I regret my sins, but I would not undo them. How can I repent being who I am?

I think about Lynna constantly.

My fingers and toes are flaking with the aftereffects of frostbite. They function, but even the slightest chill sets them to aching. I am given indoor work. Women's work. I perform such chores as are assigned to me without complaint. I speak when I am spoken to. Often, I catch my mother staring at me, her crease of caring deep. One day, as I am scouring a crusted soup kettle in the kitchen, she tells me she is worried about me.

"I am fine," I tell her. "I am healing."

"I am not concerned about your body, Jacob. You are young and strong. I am worried about *you*. You seem so unhappy."

"Everyone is unhappy," I say.

She nods. "Yes, it has been a difficult winter. Your father says we are being tested."

"If so, I have failed."

"How have you failed? Twice you have been smote down, and twice you have returned to us. You are twice blessed."

"I have been twice punished."

"Punished? For what?"

I shake my head and rub vigorously at a scab of burned food in the bottom of the kettle. I hear my mother sigh.

"Know that you are loved, Jacob. Time will heal all."

I visit the Sacred Heart at odd hours, when I can be alone with the Tree. It is bare of leaves now, with only a handful of shriveled fruits still clinging to its branchlets. As my mouth offers up prayers, I think about things that can never be. I imagine myself leaving Nodd again, following the cattle trail to Lynna's Worldly domain. She opens the door with a smile. The moment of comfort I take from this thought evaporates as she sees who I am. Her smile falls away. The door slams.

In another version of my fantasy, she sees me and smiles, and as her lips part I see the long, sharp teeth of a wolf, and I know I would bare my throat to her were I able.

Yet another winter storm comes, this one stealthily, in the night. I venture forth from Menshome to perform my morning ablutions and discover that Nodd has become a confection, frosted with a cubit of fluffy, sparkling snow. It is heartrending in its beauty, and for a short time I forget about the darkness that lies beneath it.

Soon the Village is abuzz with activity. All who are able pitch in to clear the snow from our walkways. I hear the distant drone of Brother Peter clearing the roads with his tractor, and the laughter of the young children playing in the fresh, pure snow. Ignoring the ache in my fingers, I take it upon myself to clear the walkways between Menshome and the Hall of Enoch. By the end of the day, the Village has become a maze, with walls of white on either side of every walkway and road. As I walk through this labyrinthine wonderland I see and hear the Grace at work, and I feel for the first time in many weeks that I am a part of them. *This is the true Heart of Nodd,* I think: all of us together, working as one, building and protecting and making ourselves ready for what is to come. And for the first time in months I can see a path to atonement, to forgiveness, to forgetfulness, to purity. Zerachiel may come tomorrow, or long after I am gone. It matters not. I can do only what I am able to do, and no more.

That night I fall asleep directly. I am sunk deep in my dreams when I am awakened by the buzzing of a motor. It is late. I cannot imagine why Brother Peter should be operating any of his vehicles at this time of night. I hear the muffled sound of voices from outside. Curious, I rise and pull on my trousers and boots. Will is standing outside his cell in his nightclothes.

"What is it?" I ask.

"A visitor, I think."

"From outside?"

"I don't know. Brother Jerome is out there."

I start down the hallway toward the front door, which is standing ajar. I hear Brother Jerome's voice. I am almost to the door when I hear Lynna's voice, high-pitched and frantic. "I don't care about your stupid rules. I want to see Jacob! I *have* to see Jacob!"

I rush to the door. Brother Jerome and Lynna are standing just outside the entrance. Jerome is holding Lynna by the arm. He is dressed, as am I, in his nightshirt, with hastily donned trousers and unlaced boots. Lynna is wearing a puffy down jacket and a wool stocking cap. Lynna's ATV is parked at the corner of Menshome. She has driven it right into the Village.

Lynna sees me and, with a violent effort, tears herself loose from Jerome and rushes toward me.

"Jacob!" She throws her arms around me. "Oh my God, Jacob!"

I am all things in that moment: happy to see her, startled by her embrace, horrified by her presence, and terribly embarrassed. Jerome, Will, and now Brother Aaron are all gaping at us.

"Lynna . . ." I extract myself from her arms just as Brother Enos comes running from the direction of Elderlodge, followed closely by my father. Only Enos is fully dressed. I wonder if he sleeps in his clothes.

"What is this?" Enos asks.

Lynna faces him, her jaw set. "I'm Lynna Evert, Max Evert's daughter."

Enos looks from her to me.

"Brother Jacob?"

I have no words. I am looking at my father, standing

behind Enos. I can almost hear his thoughts, his certain knowledge that I am more tainted than ever he realized, that I am beyond redemption.

The lines framing Enos's mouth deepen, and his eyes narrow. He turns his fierce gaze on Lynna. "Why are you here?"

"I'm here to ask for sanctuary," she says, raising her chin defiantly.

"In the darkest hours of the night? You drive your machine into our Village and demand sanctuary?"

"Yes," Lynna says in a voice that makes it clear she will not back down.

Enos steps closer to her and examines her face. "You are a child. Go home."

Lynna looks quickly at me, then away, and I can see the uncertainty overtaking her.

"I can't," she says.

"And why is that?" Enos's tone becomes honey smooth.

Lynna shakes her head.

"We have no secrets in Nodd," Enos says, still with the smooth voice.

I think how easily he lies.

"Why have you come to us?" he asks. "Why now?"

Lynna bites her lip and looks at me again. "I will tell Jacob," she says.

"You will tell *me,* woman!" Enos's tone has lost its honey.

Lynna is visibly crumbling. I step between them and put my hands on her shoulders. Brother Will gasps audibly at such boldness, but I am beyond caring. My connection with this Worldly girl is undeniable. Enos can only do so much.

I look into her face. "Lynna, what happened?"

She blinks, and tears course from her eyes.

"Jacob . . . I'm sorry. I didn't know where else to go. I'm so sorry."

"Sorry for what?"

She lowers her voice to a whisper. "I killed Cal, Jacob. I killed him dead."

34

For a moment, I think that I am the only one who has heard
her words, but I am wrong.

"Brother Jerome!" Enos snaps. "Bring the girl to my
office. Now!" He turns and walks quickly toward Elderlodge.
Jerome grabs Lynna's arm and pulls her after him. She looks
back at me desperately. I start after them, but my father stops
me with a word.

"Jacob," he says. "You will only make matters worse,"
he says.

"How could they be *worse?*" My voice cracks. Brothers
Will and Aaron are staring at me as if I am the devil himself.

"Back inside, you two," my father snaps at them. "Let me
talk to my son."

Will and Aaron retreat to Menshome, leaving my father and me standing in the cold in our nightshirts. He gives me a long, searching look

"Tell me what is going on, Jacob."

"I don't *know* what's going on!"

He presses his lips together and nods. "It is time we talked. Let's go inside where it is warm."

I follow him into Menshome. We take off our unlaced boots and sit before the woodstove, facing each other. I wait for him to speak. It has been so long since the two of us have talked that I do not know how to begin.

"The girl's name is Lynna?" he says.

I nod, looking at the floor. Our feet look exactly the same.

"She is a friend of yours?"

"I know her," I say.

"Is it true what she said? That she killed Cal Evert?"

"I don't know. If she did, he deserved it."

"Jacob," he says in a soft voice, "no one deserves to die."

I look up at him, and instead of seeing his usual disapproving, accusing expression, I see pain and sorrow.

"Tell me about her," he says.

And so I do. I tell him everything. I think he will be angry, but with each word I speak, I see him grow sadder.

When I have finished speaking he sighs. "Was her uncle molesting her?"

I think back over the things Lynna told me. "She said he never did. But she must have thought he might." I tell him

247

about her showing me the knife used to castrate animals, and calling it her *Cal-strating* knife.

"And this girl, who might or might not have lain with her own kin, and who may be a murderess . . . you have feelings for this girl?"

I nod, my jaw set.

"I have failed you," he says.

"I don't care."

He winces as if I have jabbed him with a needle.

"She came to us for sanctuary," I say.

"Jacob, the girl is clearly not of age. Her father will come for her, and maybe the police. They will have to sort out what will happen to her. We cannot shelter her. My greatest concern now is for you, and the price you will pay for what you have done."

"Brother Samuel can cut my brain open and make me stupid. I don't care."

His mouth falls open, and I see that I have truly shocked him.

"Jacob! That would never happen!"

"It happened to Von. And then he killed himself."

"You are not Von."

"You don't *know* who I am. You don't know anything about me."

He is silent for several seconds, then he says, "You may be right. I have been neglecting you. This is my transgression."

Hearing that gives me a peculiar sense of sick satisfaction, but it is short-lived. He continues.

"Nevertheless, you must put this girl out of your mind and beg forgiveness from Father Grace. You must—"

"Brother Jacob." It is Jerome. "Brother Enos requests your presence."

Brother Enos's office is lit by a single lamp on his desk. Enos is seated rigidly in his chair. Lynna is seated directly opposite him, with the desk between them. Her face is pale and taut. When I enter, she turns to me and almost smiles, pleading with her eyes.

"Miss Evert has demanded your presence," Enos says dryly. "Please have a seat." He waves his hand at the chair to his left. I sit down.

"Miss Evert has a story to tell us," Enos says to me, then turns to Lynna and raises his eyebrows.

Lynna clears her throat and says, looking at me, "My uncle, Cal, he came home really drunk. My dad's in Billings." Her voice is high and tight, as if she is forcing out the words. "He started saying stuff. I mean, he's said stuff before and I mostly just ignore him." She looks down.

"What did he say?" Enos asks.

She won't look at Enos; her eyes are on me. "Saying, like, how I was parading my body in front of him, teasing him and all—and it's not true! I mean, I usually put extra clothes on when he's around, just 'cause he's such a jerk. Anyway, I got sick of listening to him so I went to bed and shut my door. I figured in the morning he'd pretend to not remember what he'd said and quit being a jerk for a while, 'cause that's what he always did before. Anyway, after a while I fell asleep. When I woke up he was sitting on my bed with his hand on me." She touches her right hand to her breast, draws a ragged breath, and swallows. She is still looking at me, but I think she is seeing Cal.

"I could smell how drunk he was. I yelled and tried to get away, but he grabbed me and pushed me down on the bed and tried to kiss me." Her voice becomes a monotone, as if she is reporting something that happened to someone else. "I hit him and he grabbed my wrist and I started screaming, but I knew there wasn't anybody else home and he was pressing my wrist against my throat, so I grabbed my knife with my other hand and cut him. He fell back and he hit his head on my dresser, and after that he didn't move."

"How did you happen to have a knife?" Enos asks.

"I always have a knife," she says.

"What did you do next?" Enos asks.

"I didn't know what to do. There was blood every-where. My dad was gone. Chico was out in the bunkhouse. He was probably drunk, too—him and Cal are tight. So I came here."

"Why didn't you call the police?"

"Jacob told me that you offer sanctuary to all."

Enos sighs and moves his eyes from Lynna to me. "You two know each other well, I take it?"

"Not really," I say.

Lynna looks at me as if I have stabbed her, and I realize there can be no more deception, no more lies.

"We are friends," I add quickly. "I visited the Rocking K twice. She told me about her uncle. I met him. He was a wicked man."

"All men are wicked."

Startled, I turn to see Father Grace standing in the shadowy corner of the office. Has he been there all along? He steps forward into the light.

"How many years have you, girl?" he asks.

"Do you mean how old am I? Seventeen."

"Seventeen, and already a killer of men," Father Grace says, shaking his head.

"I'm not a killer," Lynna says.

"You killed, therefore you are a killer. According to the laws of the World, you are a murderer, and a minor. Permitting you to stay here would bring the wrath of the World down upon us. Brother Enos, your sat phone."

Enos opens a desk drawer and takes out his satellite phone.

"Who are you going to call?" Lynna asks.

"Your father." Father Grace takes the phone from Enos.

"My dad's not home, I told you."

"Do you think I do not have his mobile number, girl? We are not so backward as you think us."

Lynna closes her eyes, miserable and defeated, and sags in her chair.

"Why did *you* not call your father?" Enos asks softly.

"Cal was my dad's brother," Lynna says into her lap. "I could never tell him."

"I will tell him for you," Father Grace says. "Brother Jacob, please take the girl and wait outside." He punches a number into the phone as Lynna and I leave the office and close the door.

We stand in the hallway, neither of us speaking. Lynna's face is pale and tight. She looks scared. I am equally frightened, while at the same time filled with rage at Cal. I want to kill him myself, but he is already dead. Lynna will not look at me. She is staring at the floor, her shoulders slumped, visibly trembling. I reach out and touch her shoulder, and suddenly she is in my arms, her face pressed to my chest, shaking and crying. I hold her tight, our bodies pressed together, but unlike before, I feel no arousal, no animal urges, only our shared sorrows and pain.

"I'm sorry," she sobs. "I'm sorry."

"It's going to be okay," I tell her, stroking her back.

"I never thought he'd actually *do* anything."

"It will be okay." I say it again, but I don't believe it. I have seen the bodies of the sheep; there is no bringing back the dead.

Several minutes have passed when Enos opens the door and looks out at us. I don't care that he sees us pressed together. He motions us into his office. Lynna follows him in as if she is walking to her death. We sit in the chairs facing Enos, and he takes his place behind his desk. Father Grace is gone.

"Your uncle is not dead," Enos says.

Lynna's face, already pale, grows even more ashen.

"You injured him badly, but he is alive. Your hired man found him in your room. They are at the medical center in West Fork."

Lynna looks down at her lap, her shoulders sagging. Is she relieved her uncle is alive? I am not certain.

After several seconds have ticked by, Enos says, "Your father is on his way back from Billings. He will be here in the morning to take you home."

"I can't go back," Lynna says. "You have to give me sanctuary. Jacob told me you would turn no one away." She looks at me. "That's what you told me."

"Brother Jacob was misinformed," Enos says. "You are not of age, according to Worldly laws. Jacob will now deliver you to Womenshome, where you will remain until your father arrives. Jacob?" He looks at me with his most stern expression. "You will return here directly."

"Yes, Brother," I say. I touch her arm and lead her outside.

"This is good news," I say, trying to make her feel better. "You have killed no one."

Lynna does not reply. She looks empty and frail. I take her arm, and we slowly make our way through the Village and past the Sacred Heart to Womenshome. Sisters Dalva and Olivia are waiting at the entrance. Dalva is wearing her usual flat, disapproving frown, but Olivia welcomes Lynna as if she has found a long-lost sister. After Lynna disappears behind the closed door, I stand alone on the walkway and try to think of things I might have said.

I have no words. I am numb in all my parts.

* * *

Enos, knocking the ash from his pipe, nods slightly as I step into his office.

"This has been an eventful night, Brother Jacob." Enos sets his pipe aside and fastens his hawklike eyes upon me. "You have transgressed and brought discord within our walls. Have you considered what might be your penance?"

"I have," I say.

35

The Praying Pit is cold, and silent, and dark, the only heat a trickle of air slipping under the door from the catacombs, the only light a rectangle of lesser blackness from the high window. I see the ghost of my own face looking down into the murk, handing Tobias his pack of cigarettes. At least I am not being forced to listen to recordings of Scripture.

Huddled miserably on the hard pallet, my legs drawn up to my chest, chin tucked, the sleeves of my robe pulled down over my hands, I imagine Lynna, in Womenshome, less than two hundred cubits distant. Together, we are alone in the dark with our thoughts. Does she think of me as well?

I wake up shivering. The window is pale gray with dawn. I stand on the pallet to look out, but see only a clouded sky and part of the roof of Elderlodge. Faintly I hear the sound of a vehicle, followed by voices. It is Lynna's father, come to take her. I hear the vehicle leave. What waits for her at home? I imagine Cal, with a bandaged neck. I try to pray for her, but I sense that no one is listening, and I am soon curled like a fetus on the pallet, refusing every thought that threatens to form.

Brother John brings food. Boiled wheat, dried apples, a pitcher of water, and a strip of dried venison. He places the tray wordlessly on the small wooden table by the door and withdraws. I should be grateful for the food, but it might as well be pine bark and gristle. I eat, because I have been taught that food should not go to waste.

It is difficult to describe what it is like to not think. My thoughts are flecks of foam on the Pison, leaves blowing across a field, raindrops striking water. Several times it occurs to me to pray, but as I clasp my hands, the words flit away like gnats and I am left with nothing. I am almost glad when John returns to tell me that I have been summoned by Father Grace.

John leads me through the catacombs and up a stairway into a small alcove at the back of Gracehome. Father Grace's eldest wife, Marianne, is waiting.

"He is in the garden," she says, offering me a coat.

I don the coat and step out the doorway. Behind Gracehome is a walled garden, a small version of the Sacred

Heart, but with no Tree. The garden is covered with snow except for one patch of cleared ground about eight cubits on a side. Father Grace stands motionless at its center, his back to me, looking down at the three headstones jutting from the frozen earth before him.

"Father," I say.

He motions with his hand for me to stand beside him. I do so. With his head bowed, his long hair falls past his face, and I can see only the tip of his nose. I read the names carved into the stones: Salah Grace, Adam Grace, Von Grace. We stand without speaking for a time.

"It has been a long winter," he says at last.

"Yes," I say. There is no denying it.

"The End Times are near. Can you feel it coming?"

I feel the end is near for me, but I do not know what form it will take.

"Each of us must have his Faith tested. Von failed. The boy Tobias failed, as did his sister, and Sister Mara. There are others among us whose Faith trembles and wavers. Even I, at times, have experienced faint glimmerings of doubt." He turns his head and fixes me with his clear eye. "Does that shock you?"

"Yes," I say, for it does. Father Grace is the very personification of Faith.

"I perceive that you have been tested most severely of late."

"And I have failed," I say.

"You are a man. To be a man is to fail again and again, as

Cal Evert failed. He gave in to the temptations of his niece, the girl who came to Nodd with blood on her hands. He has paid a price and lies now in a hospital room. He will escape with his life, but his reputation will be forever ruined. It is fortunate for all of us that the Lord's capacity for forgiveness is infinite." His hand falls upon my shoulder, so heavy it is all I can do to remain standing.

"Speak to me now as a man, Jacob. Have you been with this girl as her uncle wished to be? As a man is with his wife?"

"No!"

"But that is what you desire?"

"No! I would not . . . I like her, is all. She's nice."

Father Grace steps in front of me and cups each of my shoulders in his hands and stares hard into my face. I feel my knees becoming liquid, my heart beating against my rib cage like a trapped bird. I can see nothing but those two eyes, so different, one dark and bright, piercing my flesh, the other milky and cocked toward Heaven.

He releases his hold on me and laughs. It begins deep in his chest, then spills out of him, flowing down his beard and filling the air, echoing off the garden walls and rising up like a pillar of fire. I lean back to give his laughter room, and this makes him laugh harder. He swings his arm and claps me on the shoulder, almost knocking me over.

"Young Jacob," he says, wiping his good eye with the back of his hand, "fear not. Your sins are the sins of all men. So long as we occupy this mortal coil we are at the mercy of our loins. I will tell you this: the girl cannot be yours. She is an outsider, and among her people she is considered yet a child. Were we to take her in, her people would rise up like a horde of demons from Hell. Is one girl worth risking the destruction of all we hold dear? I think not."

He grasps my shoulders again. "The Lord built these vessels we occupy, Jacob. We can fight the waves or ride them high. Some men are meant to take what they want; others are meant to follow." He draws me closer, so that our faces are only a few inches apart. "Are you a follower or a taker?"

His breath washes over me, and it is foul, as if his teeth are rotting in his head. If Father Grace is the voice of the Lord, then why would the Lord give him rancid breath?

"You cannot have all you desire, but do not lose heart. I understand the urges and needs of a young man such as yourself." He pulls me closer yet, so that his beard almost brushes my chin. "I give you my daughter Sister Beryl."

"Beryl?" I croak, nauseated both by his breath and by what he is saying. "Beryl has but fourteen years!"

"I first had Fara, who has borne me three daughters, when she was but thirteen."

I stare at him, hardly able to bear what he is telling me. From the time I was small, I have been taught that to be chaste and abstemious is to be close to Heaven, and who is closer to Heaven than Father Grace?

Breathing shallowly, I reply, "I do not want Beryl."

"Ha!" He pushes me away. "So you say now, but let your loins starve a bit longer and you might settle for Sister Dalva."

Sister Dalva is older than my mother.

"I wanted Sister Ruth, but you took her," I say, stunned by my own boldness.

Father Grace is taken aback for an instant, but he quickly recovers.

"I had wondered," he says slowly. "Ruth is a lovely child. Was this the reason you sought out the Worldly girl?"

I stare back at him. I know the answer to his question, but I am loath to share it with him. If he wants to think himself responsible for driving me to Lynna, then so be it.

"Speak, Jacob."

"I cannot," I say.

"I see." He turns to face the graves of his children. "Let me tell you how it is. The Worldly girl has been returned to her home, where she will stay. You will put her out of your mind. In the spring, when the Tree blossoms, you will wed Sister Beryl. Your transgressions are forgiven. Put the Worldly girl out of your mind. There is much work to be done. Return to Menshome." He looks at me. One eye is hard and dry, the other a moist wound. "You have my trust, Jacob. Do not disappoint me."

36

I am watched.

Father Grace has told me I have his trust, but they are watching me: John, Enos, Samuel, all of them. No one speaks of Lynna's visit to Nodd. Even Will does not ask me about her. Yet I feel their eyes on me, judging my every move.

I think about what Father Grace believes, that his marriage to Ruth drove me to seek out a Worldly girl, and I smile to myself, for I know it is not true. My feelings for Ruth were of Nodd; my feelings for Lynna reach beyond our borders and into the World. It is the difference between a leaf and a tree. I think of her constantly, in that pink house. What is she thinking? Does she hate me for failing to protect her? Is she thinking about me at all?

One day when no one is watching me I will go to the Rocking K, and I will know. Father Grace says that I am being tested. He says that the Lord has an infinite capacity for forgiveness. Can that be true? I will test His clemency with my sins. This is a concept so blasphemous, so brimming with hubris that it sends shivers through my body, but I know I must do it.

But when second Landay arrives, it is not I who is sent to walk the fence: it is Will. He tells me this as he arranges his pack. "Enos wanted to send Jerome, but I told him I was able. It has been many months since I have performed my duty."

"What about your knee?" I ask him.

"It is much better," he says, but I can see that he is favoring it.

"The Mire will be treacherous," I tell him.

"I have walked the Mire many times," he says.

I wish him well.

That night, Will returns late to the Village, dragging one mud-coated leg as if he would as soon leave it behind. He began his walk at the southern edge of the Mire, where he sank up to his waist in a bog hole. It took him an hour to free himself, and the rest of the day to make his way out of the Mire and back to the Village. His knee has swollen to the size of a melon. Brother Samuel prescribes ice and rest. It is clear that Will cannot walk the fence again.

The following Landay, Enos once again overlooks me. He assigns Aaron to the task. I am not trusted. If I am to visit the

Rocking K, I must simply slip out of Menshome at night and leave Nodd. But what do I do when I get to Lynna's house? They will all be sleeping, and I won't know which room is Lynna's. I am more likely to awaken her father. Still, I am willing to take the chance.

On the day I plan to go, I am delivering wheat flour from the mill to the kitchen when my mother opens the door.

"Jacob," she says. "It is good to see you. Are you well?"

"Yes, thank you," I say.

She gives me the look of a mother who sees past the lie and into the soul of her child. Even though it is cold and she has no coat, she steps outside.

"Jacob?" she says, leaving my name hanging in a way that demands a response.

"I am all right," I say. "Father Grace has forgiven me."

"Father Grace." She sniffs. "It is not he whose forgiveness you need. "

I am surprised by this, and she sees it in my face.

"Tell me of your feelings for this Worldly girl," she says.

"I met her at the fence and we talked. Her name is Lynna." I'm not sure what else to say. My *feelings*? I have no words. "She has blond hair," I say stupidly.

My mother laughs. "I met her at the visitation," she says. "She is very pretty."

"Oh." I am embarrassed. My mother always seems to know more than I think she knows. "I am worried for her," I say.

She nods, serious now. "Lynna is safe, Jacob. Your father and Brother Enos went with the Everts to West Fork to make sure the girl was treated fairly."

"They did?"

"Yes. Your father feared that her story would not be believed."

"He did?" I am amazed by this. Why should my father care about Lynna?

"They also wanted to let Max Evert know that his daughter is welcome here in Nodd."

My heart lurches. "Lynna is coming to Nodd?"

"I did not say that. Only that, should her situation require it, she would be welcome here as a guest. But Max Evert has sent his daughter to stay with relatives in Arizona."

"Is she coming back?" I ask.

"I don't know."

This news opens a chasm inside of me.

"Jacob? Are you certain you are all right?"

I am not all right. I say, in a shaky voice, "Father Grace says I am to take a wife."

My mother inhales sharply. "Who?"

"Sister Beryl."

"Beryl? She is barely fourteen!"

"He says we are to wed in the spring, when the Tree is in bloom."

She considers this, her lips pressed tightly together, then asks, "Do you have feelings for Beryl?"

"I do not know her."

She nods. "Jacob, have I ever told you how your father and I met?"

I shake my head.

"We were in college. He was in law school; I was studying literature. He was one of the few Jewish boys on campus; I was raised in a Christian home."

I knew that my father was once a Jew. The same could be said of Enoch, and of the prophet Jesus.

"I knew from the moment I met him that I wanted to spend my life with him. Your father had great passion and strength, and he was very handsome." She smiles. "We moved in together a few months later. Our families disapproved. My parents, who were very devout Christians, refused to have Nate in their home. Nate's mother, who lived in Minneapolis, was polite, but she hated that I was with her son.

"When your father got his law degree, we moved to Omaha, where we knew no one, and your father opened a small law practice. We talked about getting married, but for several years we kept putting it off — there seemed no reason to hurry. We had no close friends, and neither of us had any family who cared whether or not we were married. We had only each other. For a time, it was enough. And then I became pregnant with you."

"Conceived in sin," I say.

"Conceived in love. We were married as soon as I found out I was pregnant. The day you were born was the happiest day of our lives." She smiles and reaches out and presses her palm to my cheek.

"We were content, just the three of us. I became pregnant again when you were two, but lost the child in my seventh month. A boy like you. We would have named him Matthew."

"How did you . . . ? What happened?" I ask.

"It was an auto accident. Other than losing Matthew, I wasn't badly injured, not physically. But my world grew dark. I felt the loss of my baby every moment of every day. If I hadn't had you to care for"—she touches my face again—"I could not have gone on. I moved through the days in a fog. Your father made me see a doctor. The doctor gave me pills, but the fog only grew thicker.

"Then one day I was walking with you in a stroller, and you were crying, and there was nothing I could do, and I noticed several people coming out of a small church, Grace Ministries. Their faces were glowing as if they had just experienced something wonderful. The next Sunday, what we now call Firstday, I attended a service. Some of the things I heard seemed very strange, but I liked the people, and the fog did not follow me into the church. I went back the next week, and the next. Your father began attending with me. He was not a believer at first. I think he came only to make me happy.

"And then Father Grace came to the ministry, and he spoke to us. He, too, had lost a child—his son Adam. He listened to me, and he took my pain onto himself, and I knew he could see into my soul. When he learned that your father was a lawyer, he hired him on the spot to deal with some tax problems he was having with the government.

"At first, your father thought Father Grace was just

another religious fanatic, but he was a client with money, so we continued to attend services as your father provided the Grace with legal advice. Father Grace was different back then—more joyful and open and approachable. He and your father became close friends, and as I emerged from my fog, I saw that your father had been suffering in his own land of darkness, and that Father Grace had saved him as well.

"Father Grace invited us to visit Nodd, and we came, and we breathed the air, and we knelt before the Tree, and we saw the happiness of the Grace, and we knew the Truth. We saw that our life in Omaha was empty and meaningless. A few months later we moved here to Nodd, to await the coming of Zerachiel."

I have heard parts of that story before, although I never knew I had lost a brother. I wonder why she is telling it to me now. As if she can read my thoughts, my mother answers.

"Jacob, I am telling you this so that you will understand that your father and I turned our backs on our lives not once, but twice. We left our families and built a new life in Omaha, and then we left Omaha to begin anew here in Nodd. Do you understand?"

"No," I say.

"Then consider this." She puts her warm hands on my cheeks and looks into my eyes. "Father Grace is a great prophet, but he is a man. You say he has forgiven you, but the person you need first to forgive is yourself—for what you have done, and for what you must do; for who you believe yourself to be, and for who you really are.

"There is more than one path to salvation, Jacob, my son. G'bless."

With that, she returns to the kitchen and closes the door.

I am not sure, but I think my mother has just given me her blessing to leave Nodd.

In those days when He hath brought a grievous fire upon you, whither will ye flee, and where will ye find deliverance?

—Enoch 102:1

37

I cannot leave Nodd.

I have no place to go. Lynna is far away in some distant
state, and I know almost nothing of what lies beyond the
fence. I have no money, and I am still seventeen, a minor in
the eyes of the World. In a way, this is a relief, as I have no
choice but to continue to live the life I know. I throw myself
into my work, I pray before the Tree, I go on as if this is the
way it has always been and will always be. Enos must note my
change in attitude, for I am watched less closely as the days
and weeks pass.

Babel Hour is a trial. I try not to look at Beryl, but my
eyes betray me and seek her out. She is so small and thin I
could lift her with one hand. I catch her looking at me. Does
she know we are to be wed? I try to imagine life with her, but

all I can think about is Lynna. When the call-and-response is over, and the women lay out their sweets and savories, I head for the door. I cannot bear to exchange pleasantries with her. It would make it all too real. As I am leaving, our eyes meet across the room. I see that I have hurt her, but I cannot allow myself to care.

Winter moves toward spring, and we are tested again. It is a small storm by Montana standards, no more than four inches on the ground, but the snow is wet and as heavy as sand. Brother Andrew is clearing snow from the prayer wall when he is struck down. Brother Peter finds him slumped over the wall, unable to speak or move. Brother Samuel says he has had a stroke. Andrew is made comfortable in his bed, and Samuel asks us all to pray for him. We all fear that he will not live to see the Garden bloom again.

Days later, Sister Judith, Tobias's mother, is found wandering up the Spine dressed only in her nightclothes. Brother Jerome brings her back to Womenshome. For three days, she will not eat or speak, not even to Father Grace. The next day, I am changing one of the Jeep tires in the garage when a car pulls into the Village. Two people climb out. I recognize them both. The man driving is Tobias's uncle, who visited us last fall. The other is Tobias himself.

I drop the tire iron and run outside.

"Tobias!"

He jerks around, sees me, and squares his shoulders. He looks different. Taller, and more confident. I am unaccountably happy to see him.

"Hey," he says. He is wearing a puffy, bright-blue jacket and a cap with BRONCOS written across the front, just like the sweatshirt he left for me.

"What are you doing here?"

"We're here to pick up my mom." He looks past me, and I turn to see Enos approaching. Tobias's uncle walks over to meet him, and they speak in low voices.

"I'm glad to see you're okay," I say.

"Yeah, well, whatever." He is watching Enos and his uncle walk off in the direction of Womenshome. "It sounds like she's pretty messed up."

"Sister Judith has not been happy," I say.

"Imagine that." His voice is scornful. "Unhappy in paradise."

"It has been a hard winter," I say.

"Not for me," he says with a dash of his old cockiness. "I'm doing great."

"I heard you were in Denver."

"Who told you that?"

"Lynna."

He grins. "You talk to her?"

"She doesn't live here anymore."

"I know. She called me from Phoenix. She said she tried to join your cult and you told her to piss off. I told her she was lucky."

I am offended by his tone, but he is right. Lynna would not be happy living here.

"How is your sister?" I ask, to change the subject.

"She's okay. Kind of bitchy, but she was always that way. She's got a new boyfriend, so I guess she'll get herself knocked up all over again." He takes a cigarette from his pocket and lights it. "I suppose my mom will haul her off to join another cult. But not me."

His smug, judgmental demeanor irritates me. I want to shock him out of it, so I say, "I am getting married."

His eyes widen. "Really?"

"I will wed Sister Beryl in the spring."

"Which one's she?"

"One of Father Grace's daughters."

"Huh! Well, congratulations, I guess." He puffs on his cigarette.

"We will be married when the Tree is in full bloom."

Tobias laughs abruptly, then starts coughing smoke. When he has finished coughing, he looks away and says, "Good luck with *that*!"

"What do you mean by that?" I ask.

"Nothing." He flicks his cigarette into the snow and starts walking toward Womenshome. "I got to go get my mom."

I return to the garage and finish removing the tire from its rim. Ten minutes later, Tobias, his uncle, and Sister Judith return to the car. Judith is walking like an old woman, hunched over, looking at the ground, hanging on to her brother's arm. Tobias is carrying her bag. As they get into the car, Tobias looks over at me through the open garage door and smirks. It is the exact same expression he wore when I first met him.

Only hours later, Brother Samuel announces that Brother Andrew has died.

Brother Andrew and Sister Judith are not the only Grace to leave us this winter. An even greater tragedy descends upon us when Sister Ruth gives birth to Father Grace's promised son. The news travels through Nodd in sobs and whispers: the boy is premature and is born with a portion of his spine jutting out through his back. He is not expected to live.

Father Grace does not show himself. A cloud of grief emanates from Gracehome. We cannot see it, but we feel its cold, dark tentacles. Father Grace's pain is shared by all.

I am measuring a broken window in the nursery when I overhear two of the women talking. They do not see me. One of them, Sister Joan, says, "She was too young to bear a child." I can almost taste the bitterness in her voice. "It is not right."

"It is the Lord's will," Sister Olivia says.

"The *Lord?* It was Father *Grace's* will. *He* bears responsibility for this."

Olivia sees me at the window and shushes Joan; I go on with my work as if I had not heard.

Three days later, I am walking past the walled garden behind Gracehome when I hear the sound of a hammer driving a chisel into frozen earth. Another grave is being dug. A grave just large enough to hold an infant.

It think it is no coincidence when, the next day, Taylor and Joan drive off in a Jeep with their seven-year-old son, Onan. They do not return.

There is winter yet to come and already the Grace have lost ten souls: seven to the World, and three to the Lord.

38

I awaken before dawn to the sound of hushed voices and rumbling engines. I dress quickly and go outside in time to see our largest SUV pulling out of the garage. Peter and John are watching it leave.

"What has happened?" I ask.

"Father Grace is going to Albuquerque. He hopes to open a new ministry," John says. "He may be gone for several weeks."

We watch the red taillights disappear as the vehicle rounds the first bend.

"Who is with him?" I ask.

"Fara and her three girls, and Ruth," John says. "Marianne and Juliette remain behind."

"Everyone is leaving." I do not mean to say it out loud, but I do.

Peter puts his hand on my shoulder. "This is a good thing," he says. "Father Grace needs time to heal, as do we all."

With Father Grace gone, a cloud is lifted. Life in Nodd settles into a comfortable routine. Brother Enos decides that I can once again be trusted, and on the fourth Landay of February, he sends me to patrol the fence. I am happy to comply. Life in the Village has been pressing upon me, and I welcome the opportunity to spend time with myself.

It is a chilly, crisp morning as I set out. By the time I reach the gate I have opened my collar and tipped my cap back on my head. The air is fresh with the smell of sun on snow. I set an easy pace, and follow the fence south along the vegetable and wheat fields and into the forest bordering the Indian reservation. I see and hear nothing but squirrels and birds, although I see the tracks of many deer, and once the trail of a bobcat. A pair of ravens follows me for a while, making coarse remarks. They soon grow bored with my steady trudging and fly off.

As I am approaching the gully lands south of the Low Meadows, the woods fall silent. I stop and look around, but see only the scrambled winter gray of the underbrush, ranks of reddish tree trunks, and the blackish-green foliage above. I seat myself on a fallen tree, place my carbine across my lap, and listen. When the birds stop talking it can mean many things. I have learned to pay attention.

278

A movement catches my eye. I think it is a deer. At this time of year their coats are gray, and I see only a brush-crossed shadow. I remain still, waiting for the creature to show itself. Our diet has been heavy with beans and mutton of late. Fresh venison would be appreciated by all.

The shadow shifts. For a moment I lose sight of it, then abruptly it is standing in full view. It is no deer; it is the wolf.

The beast turns and fixes his yellow eyes upon me. He is close enough that I can see his whiskers and the pink tip of his tongue.

"Hello again," I say. He is thinner than I remember: coyote thin, but with a wolf's long legs and jaw.

"What are you doing here?" I ask.

He is panting, showing more of his pink tongue. He takes a few steps toward me, unsteadily, favoring one of his hind legs. I raise the gun to my shoulder. The wolf stops, not twenty paces away. I can see his ribs move as he breathes. I feel sorry for him, separated from his pack, and apparently injured. Still, he killed our sheep and will doubtless kill more. I thumb the safety off and sight in on his chest, just below the chin. At this range I cannot miss.

The smooth steel of the trigger presses against the pad of my index finger. I have fired this carbine many times, but never has it felt so alien, so deadly. I can see the wolf tense, hunching his shoulders as if bracing himself for the shock of the bullet, but he does not run. Does he *want* me to shoot?

As if in answer, the skin curls back from his teeth and wrinkles over the top of his long snout. I imagine those teeth tearing out a lamb's throat, stripping the flesh from its bones. He flexes his hindquarters to leap.

The carbine kicks my shoulder and slaps my ears. The wolf jerks back, then sinks as if melting into the snow. His head falls to the side, his yellow eyes turn to mud, and a blossom of blood works its way out from his chest. I work the lever on the carbine; a brass casing pings out, bright yellow. My breathing is loud and harsh, and the trees look as if every limb and twig has been sharply outlined with fine, dark thread. All is sharp and brittle.

Keeping the gun trained on the wolf, I lean forward and stand. Muscles straighten my legs, boots creak on the snow, lungs expel wisps of condensed breath. Slowly, stiff-legged, I approach the downed beast. I reach out with the barrel of the gun and prod his shoulder. He is dead. I squat, knees cracking, and look into his face, into the half-closed eyes. There is a putrid smell coming off him. His mouth is open. I see broken teeth; one of his canines is snapped off at the root. I use the gun barrel to roll him onto his side. His ribs are visible, his belly concave, and there are several bare patches of crusted skin where his fur has fallen away. The animal was dying. I back away. Maybe he *was* asking me to kill him, to put an end to his misery. How long had he been ill? I think back to last year. The wolf coming across the frozen river onto our land had not looked sick at all.

Nodd has killed him.

39

I hope that news of the wolf's death will bring a measure of peace to Nodd, but it is not to be. Brother Peter, upon hearing the news, calls upon Brother Samuel. He fears that the wolf had rabies and that any scavengers that come upon it will become rabid as well. The three of us take the ATV to where the dead beast is resting. Two ravens fly up from the body as we approach.

"Can ravens get rabies?" I ask.

"No," Samuel replies. "Only animals with hair and teeth." He takes off his mittens, puts on a pair of latex gloves, and bends over the wolf. "I don't think it's rabid," he says after a brief examination, "but it was in bad shape. Its hind leg is mangled and infected—looks like it might have pulled itself out of one of the traps Jerome put out. That would explain the broken teeth, too — trying to bite its way out."

"Jerome will be pleased that his work was not in vain," Peter says.

Samuel shakes his head. "To be safe, we had best not leave it to be scavenged."

Brother Peter puts me to work piling dead branches and fallen limbs into the back of the ATV. We haul four loads of wood out of the trees into the meadow and stack the wood into a crude pyre.

We then attach a chain to the wolf and use the ATV to drag it out of the woods. Samuel and I lift the wolf onto the pyre as Peter pours a can of gasoline around the base. Samuel and I back off. Peter strikes a match and throws it onto the gasoline-soaked wood. It ignites with a whoosh, sending a column of black smoke and flame fifty cubits into the sky.

We stand in the snow and watch the wolf burn. I pray for his savage soul, and I pray for myself. It is all one prayer.

Winter ends with an eerie storm that begins in the heart of the night. I am awakened by a peculiar sound. I think of men with brooms beating on the roof of Menshome. I go outside. Fist-size clumps of snow are dropping like soft white bombs, striking the buildings and the earth with audible force: *chuff, chuff, chuff.* Jerome and Will are outside, too, watching with wonder as the clumped flakes cover the ground.

By dawn the snow is shin deep, and what is falling from the sky has become frozen mist, laying an icy glaze over the fallen snow. The sky is rumbling, and the clouds are so low that the top of the Tower is invisible. Everyone who can wield a shovel is working to keep the walkways between the buildings clear. The mist soon turns to a hail of tiny frozen pebbles, and the clouds pulse with flashes and muted booms. I hear Aaron make an uneasy joke about this being the End Days a moment before a tremendous flash of lightning strikes the Tower. I feel the clap of thunder in my chest.

We take shelter in Menshome and stare out through the windows. The deafening rattle of hailstones on the roof makes conversation impossible. It lasts only a few minutes, and then the hail becomes sleet, and the sleet becomes rain, melting the ice and snow, turning the walkways to rivers of slush.

"I have never seen the like," Aaron says. None of us has. It rains for hours, and by the time the clouds lift, the snow is melted and the temperature has risen into the sixties. It smells like spring.

The promise of spring should fill me with hope, but each day arrives like a drumbeat of doom. Father Grace is still in Albuquerque, but he will return soon, and when he does, when the Tree blooms, he will expect me to wed Sister Beryl.

On the second Landay of March, I walk the fence again. When I reach the spot where Lynna and I picnicked, I discover a new breach. A marmot has tunneled beneath the chain-link again, just a few feet from where it did so before. Wearily I begin to gather rocks, but before I fill the gap, I crawl through to stand on the other side. I imagine the sound of Lynna's ATV, imagine it appearing over the horizon, bouncing and skidding along the cattle track toward me. But there is no ATV, nothing but the mating call of a meadowlark.

I find myself walking along the muddy track. I come up over the rise, and the valley comes into view. I keep walking until I can see the pink house. There is a pickup truck parked in front. I stand on the ridge between banks of melting snow and watch. There is little to see. No one comes or goes. I walk down the slope until I am standing in the yard in front of the house. It feels empty. I look through the window into the kitchen where Lynna fed me quesadillas. I see a red light glowing on the coffeepot, and an open box of cereal on the table, and a single bowl.

"Can I help you, son?"

I whirl around, so startled my soul threatens to leap from my body. For a moment I think it is Cal, but it is Lynna's father, standing quietly by the corral gate, a coil of rope looped over his left shoulder. He has been watching me the whole time.

My heart is pounding. I don't know what to say.

"You're Jacob, right?"

I nod.

"Let me guess. You come looking for my daughter." His weathered face is carved from granite. I cannot read it.

"No! I mean, yes. I was wondering if she'd come back."

"Nope."

"I just want to know if she is all right."

"She's fine. Sent her off to live with her mom's sister for a time."

"Is she coming back?"

"Not your concern, son. She's not joining up with your little cult, I can tell you that."

"I don't *want* her to join us!" I say, anger overcoming my nervousness. I take a breath and say calmly, "I just . . . If she comes back, I'd like to see her."

"See her? You saying you want to date my daughter?" He smiles at that, but it is a hard smile, a smile made of stone.

"I just want to see her," I say.

"I believe that like I believe in jackalopes, son." He tips the brim of his hat up. "Tell me something. You ever think about getting out of that cage and taking a look around? Check out what the rest of the people in this world are up to?"

I stare back at him, afraid to voice my thoughts, but he sees the answer in my face.

"That's what I figured. Evelyn told me you were a smart kid."

"Evelyn . . . Lynna?"

"I call her Evelyn, her real name. She hates it." He laughs, and his stone face softens. "Fact is, with her and Cal gone, it's kind of quiet hereabouts. How are things on your side of the fence? Hear you lost some folks."

"It has been a hard winter."

"Yeah, that it has."

"I shot the wolf."

He regards me silently for a few seconds, then says, "I suppose I should thank you. I'd have shot him myself, given a chance. But an animal like that, I'm always a little sorry to see it go. How old are you, son?"

"I will have eighteen years this summer."

He nods. "Evelyn just turned seventeen a bit ago. Well, son, I can't tell you when or if my daughter will be coming home. She's finishing up her last year of high school in Phoenix. She seems to like it better than the homeschooling we were trying to do. I ain't no teacher. She's talking about taking classes at ASU in the fall. But I expect she'll be back for a visit at least, and I'll tell her you were asking after her. I'm sure if she wants to see you she'll get in touch."

"Thank you," I say.

I kneel at the praying wall, intending to open my heart to the Lord, but all I can do is wonder how many days or weeks it will be before the Tree blossoms. I stare at the branch nearest me, almost close enough to reach out and touch. When has it flowered in the past? Sometime in late April, I think. I would ask Brother Andrew, were he still with us. Maybe Brother Peter knows.

Other Grace are gathering at the wall. I see a small, slim figure take her place at the far side. Sister Beryl. I wonder what she will pray for. To be wed? To have children? Or will she pray as I do, for the Tree never to bloom?

Our eyes meet; she looks away, and I see fear on her face, and I have my answer.

*   *   *

I am awakened late that night by the sound of a vehicle, and voices outside. I look out the door of my cell as Brother Jerome walks past in his nightclothes.

"What has happened?" I ask.

"Father Grace has returned," he says.

There will be no Convocation. Father Grace has sequestered himself in Gracehome and will see no one. Only Ruth has returned with him. Fara stayed behind in Albuquerque with her three young children. I hear from my mother, who heard it from Ruth, that Fara will not be returning to Nodd.

Every morning I kneel before the Tree, praying for it to hold back its blossoms, praying that Father Grace has forgotten about me and Sister Beryl, praying for the courage and will to face him if he has not.

Brother Wallace has taken over the Garden since Brother Andrew's passing. I am watching him one morning as he examines the flower beds, bending over from time to time to brush last year's leaves from the emerging shoots. He completes his survey of the beds and steps over the wall to inspect the Tree. He pulls down a branch and examines the tips of the twigs, then walks around the Tree, frowning. Wallace is a carpenter, more comfortable with wood that has been cut, stacked, and dried. He did not ask for Andrew's job, but there was no one else. I do not envy him the responsibility, but with so many of us gone, we must do what we can.

I complete my devotions and am leaving the Heart when I encounter Jerome.

"Brother Jacob," he says. "Father Grace requests your presence."

Sister Beryl greets me at the door.

"He is waiting for us," she says, eyes downcast. She turns to lead me down the long hall that runs through the center of Gracehome.

"Sister, wait," I say. She stops, her shoulders hunched, and slowly turns toward me. She will not meet my eyes.

"Do you know what he wants?" I ask.

She nods. "We are promised to each other," she says in a small voice. Her cheeks are red.

"Now?" My heart thumps, and it is all I can do not to turn and run.

She shakes her head. "Father says it is the Lord's will that we be wed while standing before the blossoming Tree."

"Is that what you want?" I ask.

She says nothing.

"I will not marry you if you do not want it," I say, and as the words leave my lips, I know myself for a coward, for I am asking her to choose.

She says something so quietly I can't understand her. Her eyes flick briefly to my face, then away. Realizing I couldn't hear her, she says, "It does not matter."

It is true, I realize. What we want means nothing. Not to Father Grace.

"The Tree blooms every spring," I say. "Perhaps we can ask him to wait another year."

"Father says this will be the last time. He is waiting for us."

I follow her down the hall. Gracehome has a gloomy aspect. The blinds are drawn. The air smells of wood smoke and mutton. I think they should open some windows. At the end of the hall, Beryl knocks on a heavy wooden door carved with the image of the Tree. At a faint mutter from within the room, she pushes through the door and we enter Father Grace's private chamber.

The room is even more cheerless than the rest of Gracehome. The curtains are closed, and the only light comes from two flickering wall sconces and a small blaze in the fireplace. The air is thick with the sour smell of old perspiration and something else, a yeasty smell, like rotting silage. Father Grace is in bed, in his nightclothes, propped up against the headboard, his beard spilling raggedly over his chest. Beside the bed, in a wooden chair, sits his eldest wife, Marianne, Beryl's mother. The wall next to her is covered with shelves filled with books and papers.

"Young Jacob," he says. His voice sounds normal, but he looks wrong. His nose and forehead are dead white, but his cheeks are glowing red, as if with fever.

"Father," I say. "Are you well?"

"I burn with the knowledge of what is to come," he says. He lifts a mug from the small table beside his bed. "I have been thinking of you." Sister Marianne watches expressionlessly as he sips from the mug, closes his eyes, and swallows.

"I have been speaking with Zerachiel." He says it as if Zerachiel has recently been standing at the foot of his bed. "He knows of our struggles these past months, and he has made me a promise. This spring, the Tree will blossom one last time. The Ark is coming, Brother Jacob."

Father Grace's conviction is absolute and undeniable. I hear the sound of my pulse rushing, my heart pounding. There will be no wedding-date negotiation. Sister Marianne's eyes are shining with tears. I look quickly at Beryl, who is standing beside me. Her lips are opening and closing like those of a gasping fish.

"The Ark will come," he says again, and it is as if he has reached into my chest and squeezed my heart with his thick fingers. I sense Beryl stiffen, and I sense her fear. I am no less frightened, for I believe, in that moment, with all my heart and soul, that Father Grace is speaking the Truth. The Ark will come, and I will be left behind.

"But not before you are wed." His tongue is thick in his mouth. The air in the room is so heavy and close I can hardly get it in and out of my lungs. "The Tree will flower. The boy will become a man. The fruit will set sweet and full, and it will be the last time." Father Grace salutes me with his mug. "And the Ark will come, the Ark will come." His voice is slurred.

Sister Marianne stands and takes the mug from his hand. "G'bless, Brother," she says to me. "It is time for you to leave."

There is nothing I would rather do.

40

I step out of Gracehome and take in huge breaths of the clean spring air and I know that I cannot marry Beryl, even if that means I must live out my days in the Pit, even if it means I must follow Sister Salah off the Knob and into the Pison, even if it means I must spend eternity in Hell, even if it means I must wander the earth alone until Armageddon destroys me along with the rest of the sinners.

I move aimlessly through the walkways of the Village, disconnected from all I see. The Grace go about their daily tasks: Brother Will wheeling a barrow filled with sacks of flour; Sisters Olivia and Louise in the yard outside the nursery directing several of the smaller children in a game; Brother Peter driving the ATV from the garage toward the south meadow. I have tasks of my own to perform, but I cannot think of what they might be, so I take myself to the Sacred Heart, where I am alone. I kneel at the wall and clasp my hands together and gaze into the naked branches of the Tree and pray for guidance — a sign, a miracle — for a way out. But all I see is a tree, possibly planted by Lynna's grandfather, with a scant few of last year's withered fruits still clinging to its branches.

I do not know how long my mother stood watching me, but when she kneels beside me at the wall, I sense that she has been there for some time.

"You have seen Father Grace," she says.

I nod.

"I hear he is not well."

"I think he was drunk," I say.

She does not seem surprised. "It has been a dreadful winter. He mourns the loss of his child, and the others who have left us."

"He told me that the Tree will bloom one last time, and that I am to wed Beryl, and that Zerachiel will come by summer's end."

She does not reply at first. I can hear her breathing. After a time, she speaks.

"Do you believe him?"

"I believed it when he said it. I heard it from his lips."

"Even a prophet can be wrong."

"A prophet who prophesizes falsehoods is no prophet."

"Perhaps not, but his words give us hope. That is why we are here."

"For hope?"

She nods, smiling sadly. "What will you do?"

"I cannot marry Beryl. I will tell Father Grace that the Lord has spoken to me."

"Is that the truth?"

"No," I say miserably.

"Are you certain?"

"If he has, I have not heard him."

"You must have faith, Jacob."

I hear footsteps and look back to see Brother Wallace entering the Heart, followed closely by Brother Peter. My mother and I watch silently as they step over the wall and approach the Tree. They are speaking in low, urgent voices. Brother Peter plucks a dried fruit from a branch and crushes it between his fingers. He drops to one knee and brushes aside the dried leaves and digs into the earth with his hand, then sniffs his fingers. I hear him speak a single word.

"Razar."

I know what *Razar* is. Last summer I spent a day in the south meadow with Brother Jerome, masked and gloved, applying a toxic herbicide called Razar-X4 to the thistles that had invaded our sweetgrass. The sharp, acrid smell of it had stayed on my clothes for days. And now I remember smelling that same chemical more recently, the day Lynna and I saw Tobias come out from the Heart carrying an empty bucket.

My prayers have been answered. The Tree will never bloom again.

41

I tell no one that Tobias poisoned the Tree. What good would it do? The Tree is dead. Brother Peter speculates that Brother Andrew, who could hardly see and whose sense of smell had left him, must have made a terrible error, mistaking the Razar-X4 herbicide for fertilizer. Since Brother Andrew is dead and gone, and the Lord knows he is innocent, I say nothing.

I think of what Lynna told me, that it is only a tree, a crab-apple tree planted by her grandfather half a century ago. It may be so, but I ask myself, Why did it die? Why would the Lord allow Tobias to pour poison over its roots? For whose sins are we being punished?

* * *

News of the death of the Tree travels swiftly through the Village, but days pass with no word from Father Grace. Nodd feels drained of life. For seven days and nights, we go dully about our daily tasks, awaiting the next terrible event.

On fourth Heavenday, Father Grace calls for a Convocation. This news is received with equal measures of relief and dread.

All are required to attend.

The Hall of Enoch feels enormous and hollow. The many empty seats remind us of those who have left. Elders Abraham and Seth are seated on the dais, as timeless and stern as stone lions. Minutes crawl by as we shift and whisper and wait for Father Grace to appear. Even the youngest children sense the fear and uncertainty that pervades the hall.

We have been waiting for nearly half an hour when the doors open behind us. I look back and am shocked by what I see: a man, tall and deathly pale, his head and face shorn naked, dressed in nothing but a cotton feed bag with armholes torn from the corners. For a moment I think it is Von, returned to life, but the lightning-blasted eye has not changed, and I know I am looking at Father Grace. I hear gasps and whimpers. A child starts to cry, and then another.

Father Grace is followed into the hall by Marianne, Juliette, and Ruth. As his wives seat themselves in the front row with their children, Father Grace mounts the dais slowly, as if every movement causes him agony. His legs are thin and white and hairy. He turns to face us, and spreads his arms wide.

"Brothers and Sisters." It is eerie to hear Father Grace's voice coming from this bald and shaven apparition. "The Beast walks among us."

He pauses to let that sink in. I wonder if the others are thinking, as I am, that this new version of Father Grace is the most beastly-looking thing ever to appear in Nodd.

"He spreads his poison among us—we have seen his work. He takes our people, our sheep, and now the Tree. He is here in this room, attempting to steal our souls, as he has taken the souls of those who have left us. As he took Brother Taylor, as he took Fara. How many of you have felt the writhing maggots of doubt over these past weeks and months? How many of you have suffered the wicked whispers of the serpent? How many of you have secretly questioned the word of the Lord? Look into your hearts and know that you are being tested, even now."

His eye pierces my breast, and I am certain he is speaking directly to me. I look away, unable to bear it, and I see Will, beside me, looking as stricken by guilt and shame as I feel. Even Jerome is quavering, and I realize that Father Grace is talking to every last one of us.

"Do you think that evil cannot touch you? Do you think that darkness does not dwell within you? It does. None of us is proof."

He strikes himself in the cheek with his open hand. The sound of it echoes from the walls.

"Every thought is a battle—" He slaps himself on the other cheek. Abraham and Seth are looking at him in shock.

"Every one of us is a sinner." He hits himself in the face again, this time with a closed fist, and the skin under his blasted eye splits open. "And we have killed the Tree." He swings his fist into his nose, twice. A gush of blood runs over his mouth and down his naked chin. Brother Abraham stands and tries to restrain him, but Father Grace shoves him aside and continues to club himself in the face. "Every one of us a sinner!" he cries in a hoarse voice, and strikes another blow. *"Hadeum domi!"*

Father Grace's face, hands, and chest are red with blood, and he is shouting words I cannot understand. *"Domus mortis! Malum et nequitiam!"* He drops to his knees, and the wet sounds of his fists striking his face keep coming. Marianne and Juliette are herding crying children toward the doors. Samuel and my father rush onto the dais and try to grab Father Grace's arms. He swings wildly at them, knocking Samuel to the floor. Everyone is on their feet now, and I can't see. Chairs are being knocked over. Some of us are trying to see what is happening, while others are moving toward the doors. I climb onto my chair and see several of the men gathered around Father Grace, trying to restrain him. My father and Brother Enos are on their knees, holding him down, while Samuel produces a small kit from within his robes and takes out a syringe. Father Grace is screaming hoarsely and kicking his bare feet. Samuel gets behind him and stabs the needle into his shoulder. Father Grace roars and, with a sudden convulsive movement, frees himself. He staggers to his feet and lurches forward. His eye rolls up in its socket, his body goes slack, and he falls from the edge of the dais into Brother Peter's arms.

For a few seconds, the men on the dais just stand there staring down at him, stunned by what has happened, by what they have done. Brother Enos recovers first. He looks at our gaping faces and speaks.

"It is over. You may all go."

Nearly everyone complies. I remain behind, along with a few others. Samuel puts his fingers to Father Grace's throat and feels his pulse.

"He will sleep for a time. Let's get him back to Grace-home."

Brother Peter, as stout and sinewy as a scrub oak, steps forward. I have always been impressed with Peter's strength, but never so much as now. Father Grace is easily half again his weight, but Peter picks him up as if he is a lamb and carries him out the back entrance. Samuel follows.

My father, looking after them, says, "It has been getting worse."

"It was a mistake to allow him to speak," Brother Enos says.

"What were we to do? He is Father Grace."

"The women and children are frightened."

"As am I. The death of his son, the death of the Tree . . ."

"I should have seen this coming," Enos says. "He had an episode in Albuquerque."

"I heard that as well, but it was not like this."

"No." Enos shakes his head. "Not like this."

My father notices me standing off to the side and comes over to me.

"Jacob, you should go about your business," he says in a low voice.

"Father Grace is mad, isn't he?" I say.

"He is distraught. It will pass."

"He commands me to marry Beryl."

My father does not speak.

"Beryl is a child," I say.

He looks away. "Yes."

"Father Grace commanded me to wed Beryl when the Tree blossoms, but the Tree is dead."

He presses his lips together, closes his eyes, and takes a deep breath through his nostrils. After a moment he says, "The Tree is but a symbol. It lives on in our hearts."

"I don't care. I will not marry Beryl."

He looks at me, his eyes oddly shiny. He says, "You will be of age soon. In a matter of weeks. Your mother fears you will leave us."

"How can I leave? I have nowhere to go."

He nods and places his hand on my shoulder.

"Go," he says. I think for a moment that he means I should leave Nodd, but he says, "Go to the Heart and pray. Leafless though it is, the Tree stands. The Lord will guide you through this time of trouble, as He will guide us all. Our faith will prevail."

As I walk away, he adds, "G'bless."

42

I go to the Heart. The gate is open. I kneel at the wall. I am not alone. Will is there, his bad leg stretched awkwardly to the side, his long, thin body curved over the wall like a question mark. Sister Agatha is there, not kneeling but sitting on her walker, her broken arm still bound in a splint. The unmarried Sisters Rebecca, Louise, and Olivia kneel close together on the far side of the wall, their eyes closed, their lips moving. Four of the younger children are gathered with Sister Dalva at the koi pond, kneeling at the stone bench. I have a peculiar thought: now that the Tree is dead, will we be praying to the fish huddled in the muddy bottom of the pond? And what are we supposed to be praying for? A miracle to restore the Tree? For Father Grace to recover from his illness? For the Ark to come and take us all away?

What would I pray for, were I praying?

None of those things.

I look at the Tree and I see dead branches and shriveled dry leaves. I think about the poison that seeped into its roots and oozed through its veins, a chemical made by men in some faraway factory and delivered to the Tree in a bucket by Tobias. All these things and creatures made by the Lord, all acting in accordance with His will, all known to Him in every filament of their being. Could this truly be the Lord's final test of the Grace?

If so, I have failed, tainted by the World as surely as the Tree has been poisoned. I rise from the wall and return to Menshome and take myself to my cell and think long into the night. Dawn is breaking when sleep takes me.

Jerome awakens me by kicking at my pallet.

"What?" I say, glaring at him and pulling my thin blanket higher.

"You have slept through breakfast," he says. "The sun has been up for hours. It is fourth Landay."

I groan. I had completely forgotten about my edge-walking duty.

"Brother Enos wishes to see you before you go."

I dress slowly, perform my morning ablutions, and breakfast on a leftover heel of bread with huckleberry preserves. I think of crabapple jelly. I am in no great hurry to see Enos. He will be no angrier if he has to wait another quarter hour.

Outside, a storm cloud has risen in the west, squatting

over the mountains like a great toad, while the sky to the north is a streak of brilliant empty blue. I watch the cloud, its forward edge roiling, advancing upon Nodd. I will have a long, wet, miserable walk ahead of me.

I cross the Village to Elderlodge, steeling myself for the chastisement to come. I have disappointed Brother Enos several times already, and I am not looking forward to his scolding. I know he overheard when I told my father I would refuse to wed Beryl.

Brother Enos is seated at his desk, somberly regarding his pipe, turning it in his hands, peering into the bowl at the dead ashes. His features are even more drawn and severe than usual; I sense that he slept no better than did I. He flicks his eyes at me, then points with the pipe stem to the chair in front of his desk.

I seat myself and wait.

Enos, fascinated by his pipe, does not speak for what feels like an eternity. Finally he sighs and sets the pipe aside and speaks without looking at me directly.

"Today is fourth Landay. Why are you here?"

"You sent for me," I say.

"Precisely. I sent for you because you are *here* and not out walking the fence. Why do you shirk your duty, Brother Jacob?"

"I am sorry," I say. "Much has been happening."

"You are referring to last night?"

I nod, but it is much more than that. To walk the fence looking for marmot holes seems laughably trivial.

"The most important thing," Enos says, "is that we go on. Father Grace tells us that our time is upon us. He believes that Zerachiel will arrive within days, perhaps even hours. He refuses all food and will not even permit a drop of water to touch his lips." He leans over his desk and fixes me with his eyes, and I see that his fierceness has not left him. "Do you *believe*, Brother Jacob?"

I try to speak, but the words catch in my throat, and I can only look back at him with my mouth open and my heart pounding. He holds my eyes for several heartbeats, then sits back, nodding, as if satisfied by the answer I am unable to speak.

"I thought as much," he says. "It is one thing to believe in a future that is distant, but another to embrace the reality that is tomorrow. Still, we must go on. Do you understand?"

"No," I say.

"Faith is a greased pig. The harder you clutch it, the more likely it is to slip from your grasp. We strive to believe with all our hearts in the Lord, and yet daily we transgress. The pig slips from our embrace. We sin, then we must chase it down and beg the Lord for forgiveness. Consider your recent acts, Jacob. Where was your faith when you pursued the Worldly girl? Did you truly believe that the Lord was present and watching, or did you set aside your faith and act as if He did not exist?"

"I don't know," I say, and I truly don't.

"And so it is with all of us. We believe that the Lord speaks through Father Grace, yet we ignore his pronouncements and bow to our basest desires. And now, even as he asks us to believe that the hour of our fate is upon us, we go on as if nothing will happen. As we speak, Brother Jerome is grinding wheat for bread that will not be baked for weeks, while Peter is making plans for the sheepshearing and Sister Naomi mends winter clothing for the snows that may not come until next November. We believe the End Days are upon us, yet we go on as if they will never arrive. Is this a failure, or a simple expression of the human condition?"

Is he asking me to respond? I do not know, so I wait for more.

"The answer is, we go on. Today is fourth Landay. You will walk the fence."

"It is late."

"And who is to blame? Walk what you can today. Tomorrow you will walk again."

I head toward the High Meadow, planning to begin my walk at the northwest corner of Nodd, where the fence meets the Pison. It takes me only half an hour to reach the escarpment. I stay on the narrow trail as it switchbacks up the steep slope. By the time I reach the Meadows, the sun is high and bright, and I am sweating. I stop to drink. I take off my pack and peel off my jacket and sit on a rock that looks like the shell of a giant turtle and look to the west. The thunderheads are great gray towers a mile high, boiling and frothing above a base as black as the bottom of a cast iron pan, walking on claws of lightning from the mountains to the plains. The air is effervescent; I detect the sharp scent of ozone even though the storm is still twenty miles distant.

Is this what the End Days look like? I imagine Zerachiel in his chariot of gold bursting forth, followed by the great Ark that will carry the Grace to their reward. The image is vivid. It fills my chest with wonder and awe. But at the same time, I know that if Zerachiel is truly to come, he will not be coming for me.

I look to the east. The sky is lurid blue.

I head north across the Meadows, storm to my left, blue sky to my right. The earth is spongy; blades of fresh green poke up through last year's dead grasses. Soon the new growth will take over. Peter and Jerome will herd our remaining sheep from the Low Meadows. I set a strong pace and listen to the sound of my feet, the muted crunch of dead grass, the softer squelch of moist soil. I pass Shepherd's Rock. It feels like a lifetime ago that I sat inside that stone shelter and watched my clothes dry, the same day I had a picnic with Lynna and rode her ATV.

I angle to the northwest, to where the fence meets the Pison. By the time I reach the corner post the storm is visibly closer; I can hear its faint rumbling. I turn my back on the clouds and follow the familiar path along the fence, heading east.

43

I remember all the other times I have walked this route, and the sense of safety and freedom and pride it brought me. I never thought of us as being imprisoned by the fence. It was more like a strip of armor, a strand of chain mail that made us stronger, a shield to protect us.

My fingers trail along the chain-link. The metal is cold and dry and rough on my fingertips. It is sufficient to prevent the cattle, the pronghorn, and the deer from coming and going, but the smaller creatures — coyotes, marmots, gophers, snakes, insects — pass though easily. Birds fly over it. Men can cut their way through it. It will not stop the wind or the rain or the sound of thunder. *It is a symbol,* I think, *and little more.*

Is that true, as my father suggested, of the Tree as well?

The sound of thunder is getting louder. I look back. The clouds are higher and darker and closer, and in the lightning flashes beneath them I can see columns of rain falling slant-wise upon the western plain. Above me, the sky is still blue. I may soon have to make a dash back to Shepherd's Rock. A lightning storm is no time to be standing in the open, and certainly nowhere near a steel fence. I set a stern pace and continue along the path. I think I can reach the place where the marmot dug through. The place where Lynna and I had our picnic. That will be enough for today. From there it is but half a mile to the stone shelter, where I can ride out the storm.

I am almost to my goal when the sun falls behind the clouds. The air is eerily clear. Behind and above me is shadow, and before me the greening hills still sparkle with sunlight. I see where Lynna and I piled rocks to fill the hole beneath the fence. They have been disturbed, pushed aside, and there is a pile of earth. The marmot has been busy. As I approach the spot, a cold wind strikes from the west, bowing the grasses and tugging at my clothing. My scalp begins to prickle; I can taste ozone. I look at the back of my hand. All the hairs are standing up. I touch my beard, and it crackles with static electricity. I know I should move away from the fence, but a flash of yellow catches my eye. A square of paper on the fence, fastened to the chain-link with a yellow ribbon. I reach out to touch the paper. When I grasp it, a shock travels up my arm. Startled, I let go. The wind snatches the paper and sends it fluttering off. I back quickly away. My entire body is tingling, and the fence is crackling with energy, sending out blue sparks. The first drops of rain hit. The clouds above are seething. I can see great sheets of rain sweeping down toward me. My hair is standing on end. My skin is buzzing. The grass is hissing.

"I'm sorry," I hear myself say, and the firmament is torn asunder, and all goes to white, and there is a sound like the end of the world.

I hear ringing. Not the ringing of bells, but a high-pitched sound deep inside my head. I smell ozone and the nose-wrenching reek of hot metal, burned cloth, and wet ash. I open my eyes and see deep-blue sky. I turn my head. I am on my back, about ten cubits from the fence. The last I remember, I was much closer to it, and the fence was whole. Now, for several cubits of its length, it is a twisted molten wreck.

I turn my head the other way. Brown grasses, and a marmot perched on a rock, watching me. I sit up slowly. I can feel every muscle complaining, but I do not seem to be seriously injured. The marmot whistles and scurries off. I am soaking wet. The ground is sodden and steaming in the bright sun.

Carefully I rise to my feet. My legs feel long, loose-jointed, and unfamiliar. My body aches, but my thoughts ring with painful lucidity. As I look around, I am struck by the sharpness and detail of all I see. Each leaf of grass, each droplet of water, each strand of lightning-blasted fencing stands out, blade-crisp and quivering. I look down. My tunic is singed. I am wearing only one boot. My backpack is over by the ruined remains of the fence, split open, blackened, its contents scattered. My food, a few tools, water, nothing of any consequence. I breathe in and feel the air swirling through the passages of my lungs; I feel the slow, steady pulsation of my beating heart and the heat of the sun on my face. I narrow my eyes and look up at the great orb, now halfway to the western horizon. I turn to see the back end of the storm rolling east over the plains.

Thoughts and perceptions clatter through my mind with astonishing rapidity. Was this what it was like for Father Grace, when lightning pierced his eye? But I see no angels, and the only presence I sense is the presence of that which I can see, hear, smell, taste, feel. The storm sent down uncounted lightning bolts. Was the one that struck me down a message from the Lord? If so, and I am uninjured, what can it mean? What does it mean that I have never felt so alive?

It was just a storm, I tell myself. I was foolish to let it catch me so near the metal fence, and I am blessed to have survived.

I lift the remains of my backpack. The charred fabric tears. I walk in widening circles, searching for my missing boot. I find it not far away, and near it a soggy square of paper I tore from the fence. There is writing on the paper, but the rain has rendered it illegible.

I pull on my boot and return to gaze in awe at the fence. What power such a storm must hold, that one single thunderbolt should do such damage. I climb over the tortured metal, over the molten tangle of chain-link and razor wire, and I step out of Nodd. A few cubits away, I notice a small, deliberately arranged pile of flat stones. Resting upon the topmost stone is a glass jar with a yellow ribbon tied around its top. The jar is filled with red jelly. My heart pounds as I bend over and pick it up. I twist off the top and dip a finger into the jelly and touch it to my tongue. It is crabapple tart and sweeter than honey. Using two fingers like a spoon, I scoop out more jelly and spread it across my tongue. The explosion of sweet and sour is almost too much to bear. I close my eyes, draw a shaky breath, and feel a smile spread itself across my face. I screw the lid onto the jar, loosely, and start up the cattle trail toward the Rocking K, licking crabapple jelly from my fingers as I walk, slowly, to make the journey last.

And there is hope in thine end, saith the Lord, that thy children shall come again to their own border.

— *Jeremiah 31:17*

ACKNOWLEDGMENTS

I began writing *Eden West* in 2002, working on it in fits and starts over the next dozen years with the help of several people along the way. Here are a few I would like to thank:

Mary Logue, who reminded me on a regular basis that I should not forget about this book, even as I threw it aside repeatedly and became distracted by other projects.

Bruce Anfinson, who provided enormous helpings of pad thai and shelter during my research in Montana.

Candlewick editor Deb Noyes, whose thoughtful and incisive editorial letter (with input from Carter Hasegawa and Sarah Weber) was nearly as long as the book itself, and who was entirely correct in all her exhaustive particulars.

Tobias Ball, my Latin Guy. Everybody needs a Latin Guy.

The young man who, after attending a Loft Literary Center reading of an early draft of the first chapter back in 2007, gently pointed out that I was perpetuating a negative stereotype in my description of Jacob's Native American neighbors: You were right, and I would thank you by name if I had thought to ask it.

Finally, thank you to my readers, who in recent years have tolerated more than their share of self-indulgent genre hopping, style shifting, and messing about with words: I'm having fun. I hope the same for you.